The Abyss of a Man

Gaylene Nunn

Weezie Publishing

Contents

Prologue

"One mustn't look at the abyss, because there is at the bottom an inexpressible charm which attracts us." Gustave Flaubert

Skin the color of white chocolate cappuccino. Hair so dark brown is almost looks black hangs to his shoulders in waves. Eyes of emerald green as the waters in Lake Carezza in Italy. Long eyelashes women pay hundreds of dollars to have glued onto their eyelids. A full dark brown beard accentuates full lips made to be kissed. Broad shoulders that could carry the weight of the world. Muscular arms threaded with veins that would make the world's greatest body builder jealous. Massive chest covered with a sprinkling of light brown hair. Six-pack abs a woman could do laundry on. Hips that any designer would love to have model a pair of shorts or pants. Thighs so strong they could squeeze the life out of a lion. Calves whose muscles stretch the legs of a pair of jeans to the point they might rip open. Long, tapered feet strong enough to hold this delectable body. **This is the abyss of Matthew Carson/Espíritu Libre**.

INTRODUCTION

I turn my 70 inch television off and stare at it momentarily. Why did I buy such a large TV that I rarely watch? I wonder. Because you got a great deal, my inner voice replies. I rub my tired eyes and yawn. Finally, I finished all 140 episodes of **Ama el único camino** on a popular video app. It took two weeks to watch the entire thing. Why did a fifty-one-year-old woman from Tulsa, Oklahoma, watch a Spanish love story with no English subtitles, you ask? Well, I should probably introduce myself first and then explain.

My name is Vivian (ugh! I must have been an ugly baby.) Grimes. My friends and business associates call me Vi. I'm an only child with no living family members. Married at nineteen and divorced at twenty-nine. I married again at thirty-one and became a widow at forty-five. Thanks to investments in real estate, a generous divorce settlement, and my late husband's will, I am extremely financially stable.

After two years of fighting my step-children over their father's will and traveling, I got restless. I began writing romance novels under the pen name Ivy Webber and have been successful. My last five novels being listed in the top ten bestsellers category. I submitted my sixth novel for publication a month ago. Now, I need to work on novel number seven and have no earthly idea where to begin.

I read books, and I watched movies. I looked at pictures from my travels and relived memories, both good and bad, searching for a theme for my next novel. When I came up empty, I visited several social media sites. Then I came across a Spanish TV series that looked interesting, so I started watching it. Now my Spanish is limited to yes, no, and counting to ten, but after watching a few shows, I could get the jest of what was taking place. Then I got hooked and watched all the shows. I have to admit the female lead of the show got on my nerves many times, but the male lead? Well, saying he was pleasing to look at would be an extreme understatement. Long dark brown hair, emerald green eyes, and a full beard gave the character Enrique Salas an almost dangerous, but loveable look. His body was amazing. Yes, people. Young Enrique was panty melting gorgeous even for this fifty-year-old woman.

I also loved the setting of the show and after searching the internet, found they filmed the show in Italy primarily around Rome. Being a Spanish TV show, it surprised me that the location was in a different country. Did the show give me an idea for my novel? No, but it made me want to visit Italy again.

So, after turning off the TV, me and my tired eyes grab the phone and make flight and hotel reservations for Rome for the next week. I'll check the weather tomorrow to find out if I need a shopping trip for clothing. Maybe, just maybe, I can get an idea for my novel in a fresh setting.

CHAPTER 1

After landing in Rome at 4:00 pm Friday Italy time, I spent the late afternoon and night catching up on my sleep. I've never been able to sleep on a plane, plus I had gotten up early the day of my flight to finish packing and drive to the Oklahoma City airport. After a hearty room service breakfast, I make my way around Rome to visit some of the usual tourist sites and am back in my room by 4:00 pm. Prior visits to Rome were always as a married woman, so I am curious about the nightlife. I talk to the hotel concierge, and he recommends a nightclub three blocks from the hotel. He says Saturday is a good night for people watching, beginning at 8:00 pm.

When I arrive at the nightclub, the line is long and filled with people of all ages and genders, especially females. Curious about the night's events, I join the line and patiently wait my turn. After forty-five minutes, I finally make it to the front door, where a large, handsome man stops me. He is at least 6'3" in a black T-shirt that reveals strong, inked arms. He asks me a question in Italian. I suppose I have a strange look on my face because he smiles softly and speaks to me in English.

"Do you have your ticket, madam?" his deep, sexy voice asks.

"What ticket?" I reply.

"Your ticket to get into the club tonight," he says politely.

"I didn't realize I needed one. I just wanted to come in and have a couple of drinks."

The man smiles but looks at me suspiciously. "Tonight's event is by ticket only."

Now, I'm getting frustrated. "I just flew in yesterday and I don't know what you're talking about."

"Well, Espíritu Libre appears here tonight. Everyone had to buy a ticket with the money going to his foundation," the man replies.

"If buying a ticket is the only way to get in, I will. Where do I buy one?" I can feel the anger of the people behind me growing.

"They sold all the tickets out a month ago. I'm sorry."

"Look, I do not know who that person is, what the foundation is, and I don't care. I just want a drink. Here's 500 Euros to just let me in. You can do whatever you want with the money," I say, handing the money to him folded so others in line won't see it.

"Lady, you drive a hard bargain," the man says. "Okay, go in, but don't get into any trouble and don't disappoint me." Not only does he move the rope barrier for me, but he gives me a wink and a smile. Maybe being older has its perks.

Once inside, I notice many people surrounding a platform against the wall to my right. The room is brightly lit so I can easily make my way to the bar, which is empty. Sitting down, the bartender walks up and asks something in Italian. Why didn't I learn a few words before I came? I chastise myself. I shake my head and point to a familiar bottle of whiskey with an unmistakable black label. The bartender nods and pours my drink. When he sits it down in front of me, I ask for water in Spanish. He smiles, turns around, and sits two bottles and a glass in front of me. Of course, the labels are in Italian. Ugh! I stare at the bottles and select one silently, hoping it is still water. Again, the bartender smiles, opens the bottle for me, and gladly accepts my credit card.

Finally, ready to begin my night, I turn around on my stool and gaze around the room. A few couples are sitting at small tables surrounding what I assume is a dance floor. By now, the number of people standing around the platform has almost doubled in size. I look toward the door and see the handsome, inked man that felt sorry for me and let me in. He shuts the door to the nightclub. Suddenly, loud music plays and the tension in the room rises to a fevered pitch.

Women scream something I can't understand. Many lift their cell phones toward the door and begin filming. I watch with curiosity as the frantic crowd goes wild. Soon, the handsome, inked man opens the door and four unfamiliar men enter the room, followed by the inked man. All I can see are the tops of their heads as they walk toward the platform. One man jumps onto the platform, grabbing a microphone sitting on a table. He says a few words in Italian and then says, "Espíritu Libre".

I watch as Espíritu Libre, the star of the Spanish TV show I watched, jumps onto the platform. All the people surrounding the platform go wild shouting his name and the name Enrique, his character in the show. Some women flutter their hands in front of their faces as if they are having a hot flash. Most are holding up their phones, taking videos of the gorgeous man on the platform as he waves and smiles. When Espíritu Libre sits down, the people settle down into a quiet murmur. I look toward the tables where the couples sit. Some ignore the activities, while others watch with mild amusement.

I watch as Espíritu Libre lights a cigar and takes a drink from a glass on a nearby table. Oh my gosh, he's drinking the same thing I am. I smirk a little and watch him look around the room. Even though he just arrived, he looks bored, wishing he was somewhere else. He looks in my direction and nods slightly, either at me or the bartender. I don't know which and I really don't care.

I turn around on my stool so my back faces the crowd, take a sip of my whiskey, and look at my watch. Yes, folks, I said watch. I live by the motto that simple is best. I don't need a smart watch because I don't care about my steps or my heart rate. There is no person important enough for me to drop everything and take a phone call or answer a text message. Well, there are four important people in my life. They are my part-time assistant and best friend, Grace, my publisher, Veronica, my lawyer, and my financial advisor. I don't need a car warranty or want to sell my house for cash because I don't own a house. Anyway, my four know I'll get back to them when I'm ready, not before.

I see it is 10:00 pm. It's been two and one-half hours since I left the hotel. I turn around quickly as a loud drum roll begins, followed by equally loud music. The star of the show stands and the handsome, inked man lets people onto the platform one at a time. Espíritu Libre autographs everything from books, papers, front and backs of T-shirts, chests with huge cleavage, or anything handed to him. He smiles at each person and takes a selfie with them. After about thirty people get their selfies and autographs, the star takes a break. As he sits down, Espíritu Libre looks my way again and raises his glass. I glance behind me and see the bartender return the gesture.

I look away as one man from a table makes his way toward the platform and speaks to a woman standing behind the star. She quickly turns and pushes a few buttons on a machine and the music begins. The woman nods to the man, and he returns to his table. He offers his hand to the woman seated at the table and they make their way to the dance floor. I watch as two other couples quickly join them. The music is slow and the couples dance sensually with ease to several songs before the drum roll begins again.

Instead of watching the circus again, I face the bar and alternate drinking my water and whiskey. Being alone in a bar is not the right time to overindulge in alcohol. I find my mind drifting to the couples that were dancing. Their movements were perfect. It was easy to see the way each person looked at their partner with love. It was as if they were the only two people on earth gliding across the dance floor. Maybe I could use something like that in my new book, I ponder, not noticing someone sits down beside me.

CHAPTER 2

"I 'm glad to see you didn't disappoint me," a deep voice says.

Startled, I turn and gaze into a pair of dark brown eyes first and then down at the inked arms. "Hi! I'm glad I didn't disappoint you too," I stammer with a smile.

"I'm Mateo."

"You can call me Ivy," I say. "You've been busy tonight."

"It's been a good night. Lots of money was raised for a good cause. Ivy, are you going to be here for a while? My boss would like to meet you."

"Why would the owner of the nightclub want to meet me? Was my card declined or did you tell him I didn't have a ticket?" I ask, confused.

Mateo lets out a laugh, almost as large as he is. "No, Ivy. My boss," he replies as he jerks his thumb back, pointing to the stage.

"You work for him?" Mateo nods with a grin. "I have no idea why he would want to meet me, but okay. I'm not ready to go back to my hotel yet," I reply.

"Good." Mateo waves at the bartender, smiles at me, and then heads back to his place on the platform.

The bartender places another glass of whiskey and a bottle of water in front of me. I offer my credit card to him, but he declines, so I pick up the fresh glass of whiskey and turn around to find Mr. Star of the Show looking at me. I raise my glass and mouth the words "thank you". He smiles a killer smile as the next drum roll and loud music begins.

I watch as the last group of people are allowed onto the platform for their turn with Espíritu Libre. His smile isn't as large as it was in the beginning, his eyes look tired, and he has black marks on his hands from signing autographs. I turn around and return to my previous thoughts about the dancing couples. When the music dies down, I look over my shoulder toward the door and notice several other couples entering the club. I guess showtime is over; I think. Then I turn my head in the opposite direction. Two of the new couples go directly to the dance floor while the others find tables.

"Hello."

I turn my head toward the voice and look into the greenest eyes I have ever seen. "Um, hello," I reply. "You look tired."

"Do I? Well, signing autographs and taking selfies gets pretty tiring, but it's worth it," Espíritu Libre says. "Do you know who I am?" I nod. "Really? How would an American know who a Spanish TV star in Italy is?" he asks.

I look at his lips to find a small smirk behind the mustache and beard. "I've seen your TV show, **Ama el único camino**. My Spanish is very limited, but I watched it anyway," I answer.

"Why?" he asks in a shocked tone of voice.

"It's a long story that I won't bore you with."

"What's your name?"

I laugh first and then say, "Mateo didn't tell you?" He shakes his head. "You can call me Ivy."

"Well, Ivy, you can call me Matt. It's a long story. Perhaps I'll tell you the story behind that someday. Thank you for accepting the drink. I thought you might need a fresh one. You nursed that first one all night. I was afraid all the alcohol had evaporated."

I look down at my drink and then at Matt. "How would you know?"

The bartender places a glass of whiskey in front of Matt, and he takes a sip. "Because I've been watching you like you were watching me." Matt leans closer and whispers, "why were you watching me, Ivy?"

"It's not what you think," I reply. "I have never seen a man surrounded by so many women look so bored and unhappy. When you weren't taking selfies, you were looking around the room like you were wishing you were some other place."

"Do I look bored or unhappy now?" I look into those green eyes and shake my head. "Good. Please dance with me."

"Only if it's a slow song. I can't dance these fast Italian dances."

Matt stands, and as I watch, he points to the woman on the platform. She nods and a slow song soon begins. I take Matt's offered hand, and he leads me to the dance floor. Once there, Matt places one hand on the small of my back and the other on the back of my neck, pressing my head to his chest. I try to ignore the sprinkling of chest hair tickling my nose. I hadn't noticed his partially unbuttoned shirt before now. Matt has a woodsy smell with a light citrus touch. It is unique, but not overbearing.

As soon as the first song ends, another begins. I recognize the song as a duet performed by an English singer and Italian tenor.

"This is one of my favorite songs," Matt says as he moves his hands to my arms. He gently guides them around his neck and then pulls me tighter into his arms. I watch as he closes his eyes and sings along to the song quietly. I guess he feels me watching him because he opens his eyes and stares directly into mine. The tip of his nose touches mine lightly.

Suddenly, I can't breathe and my body feels on fire from within. I know what's happening, but I feel powerless to do anything about it. This man is arousing feelings I had given up on years ago. But, he's too young for me. I just need some space. Thankfully, the song ends and I pull away from Matt. He takes my hand and leads me back to my seat at the bar.

"Ivy, have breakfast with me," Matt says as we both sit down.

The feelings of arousal are quickly replaced with anger. "I'm not that type of woman," I tell him.

"Whoa, Ivy. I'm just asking you for breakfast, that's all," he says as he tucks a stand of hair behind my ear.

"Why?"

"Because I haven't had an American to talk to in a long time. Besides, I like you. I would like you to be my friend. I don't have many."

Okay, so now, he's got that poor me puppy look that a dog lover like me can't say no to. "Okay, breakfast. Then you can tell me why I should call you Matt."

A loud laugh escapes his lips and crinkles the corners of those killer emerald eyes. "I'll have Mateo pick you up at 9:00

am. We'll do brunch, as you Americans like to call it. Now, can I take you back to your hotel?"

"No, thanks. I'll walk," I reply.

"No, you won't. It's 2:00 am and the streets aren't safe for a woman to walk alone. If you won't let me take you, at least let Mateo take you back."

"Okay, I'll agree with that. Thanks. I'll see you in the morning."

Matt waves at Mateo as I stand. He grabs my hand and kisses the top of it. "Good night, Ivy."

CHAPTER 3

I'm getting antsy sitting in the car waiting for Mateo to return. After what seems like forever, he opens the door.

"Mateo, what took you so long?" I ask in Spanish.

"So we're going to talk in Spanish now? I wasn't gone that long. Her hotel was just three blocks away," he replies.

"Yes, we're going to talk in Spanish," I huff. "What did she say about me?"

Mateo lets out a roar of laughter. "Not everything is about you, Mr. Star. Actually, we didn't talk about you at all. She asked about the weather here. Ivy said she hasn't been here in years and didn't remember."

"She's an interesting woman. I like she doesn't appear to be impressed with me at all."

It's as if Mateo can hear the disappointment in my voice. "I think little impresses that lady," he replies.

"Why do you say that?" I turn in my seat to look at him.

"I know who she is. She's Ivy Webber, a bestselling romance novelist who's probably hobnobbed with bigger stars than you."

Shocked, I ask, "How do you know that?"

"I recognized her picture from the back of her books. You really don't think I'd let just anyone in the club without a ticket, do you? Oh, here's the 500 Euros she gave me to let her in." Mateo hands me several crumpled up bills.

"How do you know about her books?"

"I read all types of books from the bestseller list. She's had five on the list and a new book coming out. They say will be a best seller too. Ivy Webber is a great novelist and I've read all of her books."

"How many has she written?" I ask, flabbergasted.

"Ten. The early ones weren't as good as the last ones, but that's to be expected. She's fantastic. She's been on talk shows, podcasts, social media, and won several prestigious awards for her work," Mateo says.

"Oh wow! I'm impressed." I pause and then say, "we need to stop at the market."

"Why?"

"Because Ms. Ivy Webber, novelist, is coming for brunch in a few hours," I reply.

"Do nothing stupid, Matt. She's a gracious lady."

"That's the furthest thing from my mind. I think it would be nice to have an American friend. Maybe she has a few connections that could get me work in the US. That's all."

I smile as I gather everything for brunch. Mateo just left for the fifteen minute drive to pick up Ms. Romance Novelist. I love to cook and have been trying out different Italian recipes, so I gave the chef the day off. There's a frittata in the oven and coffee brewing. Homemade rustico filled with mozzarella and tomatoes await on the kitchen island. There's also an assortment of cheeses, biscotti, and orange juice. After I set out the china and crystal on the island, I walk to the floor to ceiling windows. It is a beautiful, cloudless day and I can see the Mediterranean Sea. It is a perfect day to take the boat out later.

"I wonder if Ivy would like to go for a sailboat ride," I say aloud. Hmmm, let's see how brunch goes first. "I better change before she gets here." I look down at my shorts, turn and head to my bedroom.

When I open the door, I see Ivy standing by the windows. "It's a beautiful view, isn't it?" I say stepping into the living area noticing she jumps at the sound of my voice.

"Good morning, Matt. Yes, it's breathtaking. The sky is so clear and you can see a long way," Ivy says, looking over her shoulder at me before turning back to the view.

I walk beside her, noticing a slight vanilla and cinnamon aroma. She smells like my mother's sugar cookies; I smile at the memory. "Over in that direction is the Mediterranean Sea. Straight ahead is Sicily," I say, pointing.

Ivy smiles and then says, "it smells amazing. I hope you didn't go to a lot of trouble for me."

"No trouble at all. I love to cook. You gave me an excuse to try out a couple of new recipes I've been wanting to cook," I reply as I walk toward the oven to check the frittata. "This needs about five more minutes. How about a cup of coffee?" Ivy nods. "Sit down here at the island for now. I thought we would eat in the dining room."

"Matt, could we eat at your breakfast table? I'm not fancy and we could look at the view while we eat."

I stare at her for a moment. How did she know I prefer to eat all my meals at the breakfast table so I can enjoy the view? I wonder. "Of course, Ivy. Whatever makes you happy." I pour coffee for both of us and hand her a cup as she continues to stand. I can tell she's nervous about being in a complete stranger's house with said stranger.

The timer on the oven rings and I take the frittata out and place it in front of Ivy. "Let's fill our plates. You first, of course." I pour the orange juice and carry the glasses to the table. When I return, I'm surprised to find Ivy has filled her plate with a generous helping of everything on the table. It surprises me because every woman I've ever been around eats like a bird. Well, except my mother, who's almost as round as she is tall.

I take a moment to observe the beautiful woman standing in front of me. Since I didn't take time to really look at her last night, I can now estimate Ivy to be 5'6" and approximately 135 pounds. She has perfect curves in all the right places. I can see she's a little older than my thirty-one years, but age is only a number, I truly believe.

When Ivy's finished filling her plate, I mimic her and fill mine. She waits for me and we carry our plates and coffee to the table. While she sets her plate and cup on the table, I pull out her chair, receiving a warm smile that brightens her eyes.

"So, I guess you're curious about the name Matt," I begin as I sit down. Ivy nods with a fork full of frittata in her mouth. "I hope I can trust you with this because very few people know this." Again, I receive a nod. "I was born Matthew Carson to a full-blooded Irish American soldier and a Spanish mother. My mom and dad met while they stationed him in Spain. We lived in several places around the world before I was ten."

I stop and take a couple of bites, letting the information sink in. "We were living in California when my parents divorced. Dad went to his next post and my mom took me to my grandparents in Spain. My dad retired in Colorado a few years ago and my mom lives in Madrid." I pause and take another couple of bites.

"After finishing high school in Madrid, I received a football, I mean soccer, scholarship to USC. I blew out my knee during the second season so now I can only play for fun. I majored in Economics and Communications. After graduation, I got a job, got bored, and returned to Spain to study law. Again, I got a job, got bored, quit, and took a vacation. That's when I met my manager."

I take another bite and then refill our coffee. Ivy continues to eat while listening to my life's story. I have her undivided attention, which I'm thankful for. It is important to me for her to know all this history, but I can't figure out why right now. I begin again after two more bites. "Matthew Carson is not a name for a Spanish TV star, so I needed a stage name, as you American's call it. My parents always called me their free spirit. So that's where Espíritu Libre comes from. It means free spirit in Spanish."

I watch as Ivy stands and walks to the island and refills her plate. My gosh, this woman can eat. When she sits back down, she realizes I've been watching her and blushes.

"Sorry, I'm hungry," she says with a delightful little giggle. "This food is delicious and I'm honored you did all this for me."

I can feel my chest swell with pride at her compliment. I give her a big smile and refill my plate and our coffees. "Anyway, to continue this biopic of my life," I say when I sit down. "I've never been married, although I enjoy the company of beautiful women every chance I get. I try to keep my private life as private as possible, but for the life of me, I don't know why I feel compelled to tell you all this. So I'll end by saying this. My success has allowed me to create a foundation for people with Alzheimer's and dementia. That's what the ticket sales last night were for."

CHAPTER 4

I watch in silence as Matt takes another bite of food. His story is interesting, but it's his reason for the foundation that brings a tear to my eyes.

"Did I say something to upset you?" Matt asks as he reaches across the table and wipes away the tear rolling down my cheek with his thumb.

"No. No, Matt. I had a grandmother and husband that had dementia, so I can appreciate your foundation more than you can imagine. You'll have to tell me more about it sometime." I get a tender smile I can vaguely see through his mustache and beard.

Matt's eyes tear up then. "It's an awful disease. My grandmother and uncle had it as well. Now, Ivy. Let's hear your story."

I wipe another tear away first. Then I say, "I think this sharing of top secret information demands a pinky promise, don't you?"

The most beautiful laugh I have ever heard from a man parts a pair of full lips I hadn't noticed before. I find myself staring at those lips for a few seconds before looking down at my plate. Matt places his elbow on the table with his pinky finger sticking straight up. I giggle as my pinky joins his and receive a wink from those gorgeous emerald eyes.

"Where to start?" I sigh, fully aware Matt hasn't let go of my finger. I just hope what he sees in my face is blushing and not what it really is, the heat of his touch filling me from the inside out.

"My real name is Vivian Grimes. Only my closest friends and associates call me Vi and know my real name. Ivy Webber is my pen name. I write romance novels. I always introduce myself as Ivy because it's my way of keeping my private life private." Matt nods in understanding, but still hasn't released my finger and I'm burning up.

"Well, I grew up in Wisconsin, but now live in Tulsa, Oklahoma. I graduated from the University of Oklahoma with an undergraduate and graduate degree in finance. I was an only child and now have no living relatives I'm aware of. My relationship status has been married, divorced, married, and widowed. No relationship now or in the foreseeable future. More coffee?" I ask, so I can have an excuse to remove my finger from Matt's grasp and cool off.

"I'll get it," Matt says. "Should I make another pot?"

"Not for me, thanks. I'm wound up enough as it is."

"You and me both," Matt says, sitting our full cups on the table and sitting down. "Please continue."

"That's about it," I shrug.

"When did you start writing romance novels, and why?"

"I started about five years ago. When asked, I tell people I write romance novels because I have no romance in my life and live it through my characters." I can feel myself blushing. "Sorry, that was probably too much information."

"No, it's not. If we're going to be friends, we need to be open and honest about everything. I should stop there and say I would like us to be friends, Ivy, or should I call you Vi?"

"Call me whatever you wish in private, but I prefer Ivy in public," I answer honestly.

"Okay, Vi, and you can call me Matt in private and Spirit in public. I know Espíritu can be hard to say." The heat inside returns as I get a wink and a big smile with the comment. "Are you finished eating?"

"Yes, thank you. It was delicious. Please let me help you clean up."

"No, the housekeeper will do that." Matt pauses for a few seconds. I feel he's struggling internally with something, but then he looks me directly in the eyes. "Vi, do you have plans for today?"

"No, not really. The concierge said the shops are closed today, so I thought I would just wander around a bit."

"It is a beautiful day, and I want to take my sailboat out. Please come with me. I'd enjoy the company."

I look down for a few seconds at my sundress and sandals I chose to wear today. When I look up, I see those sad puppy dog eyes. "Do you promise you're not a serial killer that will dump my body in the ocean never to be found?"

"Oh my lord, you are a novelist, aren't you?" Matt asks with a huge grin. I can't help but roll my eyes at him. "Give me a few minutes to change and make a couple of phone calls." I nod and head back to the windows to look out over the beautiful view from Matt's penthouse apartment. Change he said? I never got past his face to even know what he was wearing. Crap, if we're going to be friends, I need to control my thoughts, feelings, and body.

CHAPTER 5

I stop quickly as I step through the doorway of my bedroom. Vi is standing by the windows, staring at me. Her eyes are as big as saucers. Confused, I stare back, wondering if she's concerned about my clothes. Then I realize she's staring at the duffle bag in my hand.

"Don't be concerned about the bag. It's just a couple of chains, some rope, and duct tape." I try to sound serious but fall short. I walk over to her and brush her cheek with my fingertips. "It's okay, sweetheart. It's only a change of clothes for me in case I want to swim and jackets for both of us. I don't want you to get cold."

"Oh, okay," Vi replies timidly, blushing.

I take her hand in mine and say, "well, I see one thing this friendship needs to work on first is trust. I'll take care of you, Vi, just like I will your secrets."

It only takes a couple of minutes to go down the elevator to the back door of the apartment building where the car waits. Vi looks confused again, so I explain. "On weekends, reporters flock to the front door waiting to see if I or a woman leaves the building. Mateo is out front waiting with the SUV to confuse them and give us time to leave unnoticed."

"I'm impressed," Vi says. "I had heard the reporters could be ruthless."

"These are more nosy than ruthless. If I throw them a crumb once in a while, it satisfies them for a few days."

"Wow! This boat is amazing," Vi says excitedly when we walk up to the boat.

"Thanks. This is one of my favorite ways to relax. Let's get you on board and I'll show you around." I jump on board, drop the duffle bag on the deck, and reach for Vi. Although I intended to grab her by the hands, I somehow ended up with my hands on her waist, lifting her up and onto the boat. I am surprised how light she is and pull harder than is necessary.

Vi ends up firmly pressed against my chest with my hands still on her waist. The heat from her body feels great against me and when I look down at her, I notice the deep blue of her eyes for the first time. They seem to pull me into a space of warmth and happiness that I hadn't felt in years. No, no, no, my mind screams at me, so I set her down beside me quickly.

"Let's go," I say, picking up the bag and turning away from her, almost panting. I reach for her hand and lead her below deck, where I point out the gallery filled with enough appliances to make a gourmet dinner. Next, we pass by the bathroom and enter the bedroom. I spent extra money on the boat so I could have an almost full size main bedroom complete with king bed and a sofa.

"Matt, this is very nice. I think this is bigger than my bedroom back home. Do you actually get to sleep here?" Vi asks, looking around the spacious room.

"Sometimes, I do, though not as often as I would like. Mateo comes with me sometimes because it is a two-man operation to get all the sails hoisted. I let him know we were going out, so he stocked the fridge with snacks and drinks earlier. Let's grab some water and get going. You ready?" I ask turning around to face Vi.

"More than ready," she answers with excitement, and I am blessed with a smile that could rival the sun. I take her hand, stop by the fridge for two bottles of water, and lead her up on deck. "What do you want me to do, captain?"

"Well, as my first mate, you need to sit down behind the wheel and wait for me to untie the ropes," I answer with a grin. I lift Vi up and place her in the captain's chair behind the wheel. I jump off the boat and untie the ropes. Then I throw them onto the boat, before jumping back on myself. Next, I move to the wheel and start the engine while Vi looks on curiously. After letting the engines warm up for a few minutes, I engage the engines and move the throttle just enough so the boat eases away from the dock. Once we clear the dock, I increase the speed a little, but not enough to create unnecessary waves to rock the remaining boats.

"Come and stand between me and the wheel," I tell Vi. She jumps out of the chair and does what I say. There's barely a hand's width of space between her and me when she does. "Place your hands on the wheel for a minute." When I feel Vi hesitant, I tell her it's okay, and she does.

I reach up and gather her beautiful red mane in my hands. She has a slight shiver to her body when I touch her neck. Well, that was interesting, I think. I wonder if she's chilled already. I wind her hair into a bun and then fasten it with a hairband from my wrist. Then, I do my hair.

"That will keep the hair from our eyes," I say, leaning over to whisper in her ear. I take a moment to inhale Vi's sweet scent of vanilla and cinnamon, once again noticing her shiver. "Are you getting cool?" She shakes her head no. "Great, let's go to sea."

"Should I sit back down?" Vi asks, leaning back so I can hear her soft voice over her head and shoulder.

"No ma'am. You are going to learn to steer this thing so I can put up the sails later."

"You're kidding right?"

"No, I'm not kidding," I answer, leaning in and feel the shiver again. Hmmm, is there something I'm missing here? I ask myself. By now, we are far enough from the dock to speed up the boat. I slowly ease the throttle forward and place my hands on top of hers on the wheel. I lay my chin on her shoulder so she can hear me and take notice of how creamy Vi's skin looks and feels.

With my hands still covering hers, I move them to the correct location on the wheel. I explain the workings of the throttle, the automatic radar plotting aid, other gauges and dials, and the autopilot. Much to my surprise, Vi listens intently and asks extremely good questions.

As she watches, I turn the boat to leave the Italian coastline and head toward the Mediterranean Sea. I speed up the boat and we race forward on the course in set on the gyrocompass. Per my instructions, Vi watches the gyrocompass and looks forward navigating the boat. It takes several minutes for her to realize I removed my hands from hers and she was actually steering the boat alone.

When it finally dawns on her, Vi turns her head and smiles at me. "Matt, am I really steering the boat?" I nod, smiling at her excitement. "This is great!" she yells.

"Okay, sweetheart, just a little further, and then you're on your own so I can unfurl the sails. Let me show you what to do." I explain the steps she needs to take as I unfurl each sail. I give her a hand signal that I will use when she needs to proceed to the next step. "Are you ready?" I ask, stepping out from behind her.

"More than ready, captain," she yells.

"Good girl," I say, leaning in to kiss her on the forehead before moving away.

One by one, I unfurl the sails and Vi does exactly as I instructed. As I make my way back to her, I feel the boat lurch forward when Vi turns off the engines.

"What do we do now, captain?" Vi asks when I reach her.

"You did great, Vi. Now we sit back, relax, and watch the scenery as we go past." I hop into the oversized chair behind her, spread my legs wide, and lift Vi into the vacant space. With one hand on her waist so she doesn't fall off the chair, I point out various places we pass with the other.

I can tell Vi is thoroughly enjoying every moment, which relaxes me even more. I feel the tension of the last few weeks slowly leaving my body. Now I realize inviting her along was the best decision I've made in a long time. Well, second best decision. The first best was talking to her last night.

After approximately two hours of sailing and no land in sight, I yawn. "I think we've gone far enough. I'm going to bring the sails in and anchor here for a while. Are you okay with that?"

"I am. I think the best brunch chef in Italy needs a nap," Vi replies with a soft smile.

"Would you mind, Vi?"

"Not at all. I'm just going to sit here and enjoy the beauty of the sea and sky."

After taking care of business, I head below to the bedroom and fall asleep as soon as my head hits the pillow.

CHAPTER 6

I wake up with a jump. I guess I dozed off sitting in the chair with no intention of doing so. The boat is quiet, so I know Matt is still napping. I sneak down into the galley and grab a fresh bottle of water. Walking up the steps, I look up and see a dark cloud in the distance. "Oh my gosh, I wonder if that's a storm," I say aloud. I rush back down the steps and set the bottle of water on the counter. Then I rush into the bedroom where the most breathtaking sight lies asleep on the bed.

Matt removed the hairband from his hair so his dark brown locks are scattered across the pillow. Long lashes lie on his top of his cheeks. The white T-shirt is stretched across his chest, showing muscles that would make a Greek god envious. Muscular arms with large veins lie on each side of Matt's body, ending in powerful hands with long fingers. The T-shirt hides what I assume is a narrow waist and his knee-length shorts hide his thighs. Even in his sleep, muscles that football players would pay dearly for define the calves of his legs. Long tapered feet with well-manicured nails complete the look.

My body heats instantly at the sight of this gorgeous man. My heart rates increases rapidly as I remember those powerful arms wrapped around me last night when we danced. Feelings of desire long suppressed scream to be released onto the bed next to Matt. Why did I come down here? I ask myself. Oh yeah, right. There's a storm.

I lean over the bed and touch Matt's shoulder softly. His eyes open slowly and his emerald stare fixates on me for a moment. "Matt, I think we have a problem," I whisper. "It looks like there's a storm on the horizon."

Matt reaches up and strokes my cheek. "We'll be fine, sweetheart. Now, let's go up and see what we have to deal with." He doesn't hurry as he sits up, slips his sneakers on and pulls his hair back. Matt grabs my hand and leads me up on deck.

First, Matt scans the horizon, looking at the clouds moving toward us. Next, he lifts me into the captain's chair behind the wheel. Then, he turns up the volume on the radio he muted before taking his nap. The conversation is all in Italian, so I don't know what they say, but it is brief.

"Fortunately, it's not a storm, but fog because it's that time of year," he tells me. "There's no predicting when it will happen. Let's get busy. Okay? I'm going to turn the boat around and set our course. I need you to steer while I put out fog lights. We will need to move fast."

"I'm ready," I reply, trying to keep my voice steady.

Matt starts the engines, turns the boat around, and sets the course. He leaves me to man the wheel. I'm too busy concentrating on keeping the boat on course to watch him. I don't know how long we've been moving or when the tears began rolling down my cheeks. I just know when I feel Matt slip behind me and fold me in his arms, holding me against his firm, broad chest. His hands then cover mine on the wheel.

"Sweetheart, don't cry. We're going to be okay. There's no reason to be scared," he whispers in my ear.

"I'm not scared as long as I'm with you," I reply as the tears flow harder and faster. "It's my fault. I dozed off when I should have been watching."

"Vi, it's not your fault. Things happen," Matt says, moving one muscular arm around my waist. I feel him look back over his shoulder before reaching for the radio. Once again, the conversation is in Italian and brief. "Vi, we won't be able to make it back to Rome, but we need to get out of the Mediterranean Sea, so we're not in a shipping lane. I hope you don't have plans for early tomorrow morning, because we are spending the night on the boat and probably part of the morning until the fog clears. I estimate we have another thirty minutes before we have to stop. Why don't you go down to the galley and make us something to eat while I finish up here?"

I release the wheel and turn to leave, but Matt's massive arm still surrounds my waist. He pulls me to him and places a soft kiss on my forehead before releasing me.

CHAPTER 7

Finally, we are out of the sea and shipping lane area. The timing is perfect because I can no longer see the front of the boat. I cut the engines off and drop the anchor. I'm happy Vi could steer the boat so I could get all the lights out and turned on. The woman is amazing because she never whined or cried about the circumstances. She just shed her tears because she blamed herself for the situation. Taking deep breaths of the fog filled air, I think about the other women I have been with in the past. In this situation, all would have been scared, complaining, or calling their daddies asking for help. With a smile on my face, I start the generator before heading down to the galley.

Thankfully, Mateo stocked the galley well, and Vi has laid out freshly sliced bread, cheeses, and a variety of sliced meats. The galley smells of basil and garlic, but I don't see any. Vi has the table set and is pouring the wine when I finish washing up in the bathroom.

"This looks delicious, Vi," I say as I sit down. "But I smell basil and garlic. Did you cook something?"

"No," she replies as she sits down. "Have you ever had dipping oil before?" I shake my head. "Well, I have it a lot when I'm not sure what I want to eat. It's a mixture of olive oil, basil, garlic, and a few red pepper flakes." Vi picks up a small bowl containing the mixture. "Are you willing to try it?" she asks, raising one eyebrow.

I watch as she tears a small bite from a slice of bread, dips it into the concoction, and opens her perfect pink lips. I watch mesmerized as Vi places the bite in her mouth and licks those lips. My entire body tenses at the scene and grows hot. I look down in a rush, trying to focus on the fact that Vi is now handing me the bowl. Grabbing the bowl from her, I follow her lead and place a dripping piece of bread in my mouth. The problem is that my mind is still on her lips and I dribble the dipping oil down my chin first.

Vi giggles, leans over, and wipes my chin with her fingers. "I forgot the napkins," she says, jumping out of her chair blushing. Okay, no big deal and certainly not worth blushing over, I think to myself. "Do you like it?" Vi asks as she sits back down and hands me a napkin.

"It's very good and goes perfectly with this meal," I grin while she watches me. "What?"

"I would like to see your lips so I could tell if you're grinning or smirking. Women must think your long mustache hairs tickle when you kiss them."

Whoa, what a comment, I say to myself. "No one's ever complained, if that's what you're suggesting. I guess they were preoccupied with other things when I kissed them," I reply, jiggling my eyebrows. We generalize the rest of the meal with small talk. LOL!!!

After dinner, I insist on helping Vi cleanup, even though the gallery is barely large enough for one person. Our bodies constantly brush up against each other, leaving me breathless. At one point, I have to excuse myself, go to the bathroom, and splash cold water on my face and neck.

When I return, Vi asks about going out on the deck to see the fog. Concerned that she may be claustrophobia, I truthfully tell her we need to keep the cabin closed up, so the humidity does not get inside.

"What shall we do?" Vi asks.

"Why don't we play poker? I have cards and chips. Mateo and I play to pass time when we are on the boat," I reply.

"Hmmm. I don't know, but I guess we could try," Vi says in a strange voice. I reach into a cabinet and pull out the cards and chips.

"What would you like to play?" I ask sitting down and dividing up the chips.

Vi concentrates for a few moments and then says, "Texas Hold Em." I watch as she grabs my sunglasses off the counter and sits down. I get a funny feeling that her innocence is just a tease. "What should we play for?"

"Winner gets to sleep in the bed. Loser sleeps on the sofa," I say with a grin. Vi nods and I deal the first hand.

Two hours later, I know I've been had. Vi sits across from me with my too large for her face, sunglasses hiding her eyes. The stack of poker chips in front of her is twice the size of mine. She tries to hide the fact that she's getting sleepy, but I've noticed several tiny yawns escape her beautiful lips.

"Last hand," I say. I'm getting tired too. Vi nods her head in agreement. I deal the cards and have a poor hand, but I want Vi to win so she can have the bed. "All in," I say, pushing my meager stack of chips to the middle of the table. Vi takes several seconds to decide what she wants to do before pushing her stack of chips next to mine. When the hand is complete, I end up winning all the chips and the bed.

Vi removes the sunglasses, rolls her eyes and giggles. "I lose. Shall we finish the wine while we put everything away?" I nod as she stands, grabs the glasses and fills them. When she sits down, I have the table cleared.

"Vi, why did you come to Rome?"

She sighs heavily and then answers my question. "I'm under contract to deliver another book to my publisher in nine months. Ideas for novels come easily for me, but I've run into a blockage. I'm totally at a loss, so I thought a change might help. I fell in love with the areas your TV show was filmed in and I thought if I visited those, they may spur some ideas."

"That show was three years ago and a lot of it was staged, but I think I know a few similar areas that you could visit. I could take you there if you like."

"Matt, I appreciate it, but I know you're busy with your foundation work and public appearances. Perhaps you could just point them out on a map and I'll take it from there."

"No, I insist. I will make time to take you there. That's what friends do for friends. Now, finish your wine and let's go to bed." I take the last sip of my wine and head to the bedroom. I'm laying a blanket and pillow on the sofa when Vi enters the room. "There are new toothbrushes in the bathroom," I tell her. I rummage through my duffle bag and toss her my T-shirt. "You'll sleep more comfortable in this."

"Thanks. I'll just be a minute," Vi replies, carrying the T-shirt to the bathroom.

When she returns, I have my back to the sofa. Once I hear her lie down, I head to the bathroom to take care of my own needs. Vi is sleeping soundly when I step out of the bathroom. I turn off all the overhead lights, leaving only a soft light from the lamp next to the bed. Sitting on the side of the bed, I look at the sleeping beauty across from me. Her red hair looks like embers laying across the pillow. Her pink lips are slightly parted as she breathes deeply.

I can't bear the idea of her sleeping on that hard sofa. I stand, gently lift her and place her on the opposite side of the bed. Vi instantly turns to her side, facing the center of the bed. I walk around the bed and crawl in. There's plenty of vacant space between us, so she shouldn't feel uncomfortable if she wakes. Turning toward Vi, I watch her as she sleeps. Something foreign stirs inside me. I want to protect her and have her near me. That's what friends do, right?

CHAPTER 8

S omething is tickling my nose, and it wakes me. Without opening my eyes, I reach up and rub my nose. But the tickling doesn't stop when I stop rubbing. I slowly open my eyes to find my head resting on Matt's shoulder and it's his chest hair tickling my nose. What the heck? I went to sleep on the sofa. How did I get into his bed with my head on his chest, his arm around my waist, and one of his legs lying across mine? Did he put something in my wine glass? No, he didn't touch my wine glass. I have to get back to the sofa without waking him.

I gently ease out from under his leg first and then slowly lift his arm, laying it across his waist. So I lift my head and ease backwards. Just as I begin to turn away from Matt, his hand grabs my arm.

"Please don't go. I haven't slept this peacefully in years," Matt says in a soft voice, pleading for me to stay. "I promise I won't bother you."

"Okay," I reply, lying down with my back toward him. In a few seconds, I hear his soft breathing and close my eyes.

The smell of bacon arouses my sleeping brain and my stomach growls. I can't now and will not ever be able to resist bacon. They will bury me with a piece in my hand. I smile and think I need to add that to my will. I stretch and realize I'm in

Matt's bed alone. Reaching over, I pull his pillow to me and inhale his scent. OMG! I have to get over this attraction stuff. He wants to be friends, and that's it. My animalist feelings will only end this friendship before it really gets off the ground. I climb out of bed and stand in the doorway leading into the gallery where Matt's back is to me.

"Omelets will be ready shortly," he says without turning around.

"How did you know I was standing here?"

"I can sense when you're nearby. Ready for a cup of coffee?" Matt asks as he turns around.

I inhale sharply as I take in the man standing a few feet away. This is the first time I've seen him without a shirt. He has broad shoulders that could carry the weight of the world. His muscular arms are threaded with veins that would make the world's greatest body builder jealous. Matt's massive chest is covered with a sprinkling of light brown hair. Below are six-pack abs a woman could do laundry on. Any designer would love to have his hips model a pair of shorts or pants. A "V" leads downward to dangerous territory. I slowly raise my eyes up to his, only to find his gaze taking in the full length of me.

"Uh, I better change before I have that coffee," I stammer.

"Why? The view from here is gorgeous," Matt says.

I can feel my body almost combusting and I turn on my heels, grabbing my dress and underwear as I make my way to the bathroom. Once dressed, I look down at Matt's T-shirt. It is almost threadbare. I run my hand into the T-shirt and find that it is practically see through. How did I not notice that before? Well, for one, there are no real mirrors on this boat and second, you were so tired last night, you never thought about it when Matt handed it to you. Of all the nights, to strip completely naked before putting on the shirt you picked last night, my mind says. That means Matt saw me, all of me. OMG! I'm horrified that he would ever see my old as his mother's body. There goes anything more than friendship, my mind says.

I take a deep breath to tamper my embarrassment and dig deep to find some self-respect before leaving the bathroom. I toss the threadbare T-shirt on the bed as I pass and enter the galley.

"You're just in time," Matt says, as if nothing ever happened. He places our plates on the table and sits down across from me. "Toast? I didn't find any jam or jelly, but I like a ton of butter on mine, so I hope you do, too."

"I do. Thank you."

Matt reaches across the table and lifts my chin with an index finger. "Vi, look at me," he whispers, and I do. "I'm sorry if I embarrassed you. You are a beautiful woman and 100% all natural. You are a genuine treasure."

I can't help but smile wistfully. "You mean antique."

"No, I said treasure, and I meant it. You are something special and someone a person like me needs to hold near to their heart," Matt says in a soft voice. "Age is a number on a piece of paper that can control our lives if we let it. You don't let it control you physically, so don't let it control you emotionally." He brushes my cheek with his fingertips and smiles. Then he picks up his fork and begins eating.

I do the same, promising to commit his words to memory and consider them later for whatever reason.

CHAPTER 9

I hope I eased Vi's embarrassment. I truly didn't intend to upset her, but when I saw her in that T-shirt, I almost passed out. Taking another bite of my omelet, I look down at my plate. Thinking back, I didn't realize I had picked up one of my oldest worn T-shirts when I threw it in the duffle bag, but boy, am I glad I did. Vi might as well have been nude, and I loved everything I saw.

Unlike all the women I have been with, there is nothing fake or surgically altered on her body. I bet on closer inspection (and I would really like to do the inspection personally) there are no scars. Matt, what are you thinking? my mind yells. You are the one that wanted to be friends. Don't blow it now with your dirty thoughts and feral instincts. We need to change the subject and do it now!

"Vi?"

"Yes?"

"You haven't asked me questions the whole time we've been together. Why is that?"

I watch as a tiny "V" forms between her eyebrows and she's quiet. When she finally speaks, her voice is soft. "I don't want to pry into your life. I want you to tell me whatever you want me to know. You suggested we be open and honest in our friendship. I trust you to do that, and I hope you will trust me as well."

"Good point. I do trust you, Vi."

"Well, since we are being open and honest, how did I end up in your bed?" she asks with a twinkle in her eye and a smirk.

"You fell asleep quickly and I know the sofa is as hard as a rock. So once you were in a deep sleep, I picked you up and put you in the bed. You never woke up," I reply.

"Why did you ask me to stay?"

"I told you the truth. I haven't had a peaceful night's sleep in years. My mind won't stop working. I tried different things, but they don't work for me. Last night, I looked at you, closed my eyes, and that's all I remember until you tried to get up. So, thank you for a good night's sleep."

"You're welcome and thank you for allowing me to sleep in your soft bed. Now, I'll clean up and you do whatever you need to do," Vi tells me.

After a quick shower, I slowly open the hatch and see the boat is still covered in fog, but the light from the sun is getting brighter by the second. I duck back down and close the hatch. Vi is sitting at the table, looking at her phone with a frown on her face and her chin resting in one hand.

"Everything okay?" I ask.

"Yeah, just peachy," Vi answers, but I detect anger in her voice.

I pull her hand away from her chin, which makes her look at me. "Okay, Vi. Just peachy sounds like the southern version of fine and we both know when a woman says fine, it's not a good thing." Her laughter fills the galley. It's infectious and before I know it, we both have tears running down our cheeks from laughing so hard. Finally, the laughter subsides and we both wipe our tears away.

"Talk to me, sweetheart," I weakly manage to say.

"I just got a text from the hotel. I didn't know how long I would stay in Rome and booked my room through Wednesday. Yesterday, I requested an extension, but apparently, there is some big event next weekend in Rome. I need to be out of the hotel by Thursday morning. All the decent hotels in Rome are already booked up. So I either need to find a cheap hotel or leave Rome temporarily. Just peachy, huh?" Vi replies, rolling her eyes. "Can you recommend a little out of the way place I could stay until I can get back in the hotel?"

"First, the big event is the equivalent of the Oscars." I pause for a minute, trying to think of another place, but then my body takes over my mouth. "I do know the perfect place for you to stay. It's close to the hotel and I know there are vacant rooms."

"Really? What's the name of the place so I can call it when we get back?"

"The name of the place is Matt's penthouse suite. There are two vacant bedrooms, but they share a bathroom," I answer with a grin.

"Oh, Matt, that's sweet, but I can't impose on you like that," Vi quickly responds.

"I would love for you to stay there. Besides, Mateo and I have to leave later this afternoon and won't be back until Friday night. I am attending the event Saturday night, so we will see very little of each other."

"Are you sure? I will leave as soon as the hotel has rooms available, I promise."

"I'm sure. Please stay as long as you like. It's nice having you near me. I feel," I pause searching for the correct word. "I feel normal."

"Okay, but if I get in the way, please be honest and tell me. It won't hurt my feelings," Vi says.

"Great. Let me have your phone and I'll program my number in. I'll have someone pick you up at the hotel Thursday morning and take you to the apartment. My housekeeper can show you the vacant rooms. She doesn't speak English, but I'll work things out with her beforehand."

Vi hands me her phone and says, "Matt, thank you. I'm not ready to leave Rome yet and the thought of leaving and coming back was weighing heavily on my mind."

I look into her earnest face. My mind says the third best idea, punk, and I know everything will work out. "Here's your phone. Text or call me any time you have questions or need anything. Okay?" I receive a nod from Vi that makes my heart smile.

CHAPTER 10

It is 2:00 pm when we arrive at the dock. Matt had Mateo meet us at the dock to take me to the hotel. Matt had to go to his apartment and pack for his road trip to Naples, Bari, Palermo, and several stops in between.

"Ivy," Mateo starts off tentatively when he starts the car. "I know who you are and I'm a big fan of yours. I've read all your books, even the early ones."

"Wow, Mateo. Thank you. My next one should be out by next week."

"I can't wait to read it."

"I have a book due to my publisher in nine months and I'm out of ideas. I had hoped coming to Rome would jumpstart my creative juices. Mateo, did Matt tell you I would stay at the apartment for a few days?"

"Yes, ma'am, he did. Unfortunately, Antonio, the other security guard, will be with Matt and I, but I'll make sure a reputable person picks you up."

"Mateo, do you have paperbacks or hard backs?" I ask.

"Paperbacks only. I couldn't find them in hardbacks here," Mateo answers. "Well, here we are. I'll see you when we return. I guess I should tell you, Antonio and I live in the apartment, too."

"Thanks, Mateo," I say as he opens my door. "Just between us. My real name is Vivian and my friends call me Vi. Since we're friends now, no more Ivy unless we're in public, okay?" I wink at him. My huge, handsome, inked friend kisses my hand and winks back before closing the door behind me.

I step into my room, tossing my purse on the bed. A thought hits me and I dig my phone out to find a new message. I look at the phone and discover I hadn't taken it off mute since I left the hotel for the nightclub. I open the message to find "I miss you already". The sender is Matt. With a smile on my face and a strange warmth in my heart, I reply with a thumbs up emoji.

I stare at the message for a few seconds. Then I remember what I was going to do. I text my assistant, asking her to send first edition hardbacks of all my books, including the newest one, to Matt's address in my name. I instantly receive a reply from her telling me my new book is #10 on the bestseller list this week for pre-sales and climbing. No pressure on the next one, huh?

Thursday morning, I'm up early packing the last minute items for my move to Matt's apartment. Other than the code for the penthouse's elevator and his door, I haven't heard from him. I didn't expect to. It's not that kind of relationship, is it? Since Mateo dropped me off at the hotel, I've wandered the streets of Rome and surrounding small towns. Still, I'm no closer to an idea for my novel. The phone in my room rings as I close the last suitcase.

"Ms. Webber, there is a gentleman here for you," the concierge informs me.

"Thank you. I've been expecting him. Would you send someone to retrieve my luggage?"

It only takes a few minutes before a porter knocks on my door. She gathers my two suitcases and follows me to the elevator. When reaching the lobby, the concierge meets me at the elevator with my driver. I heavily tip the concierge and porter while the driver picks up my luggage. Then I follow him to the car. We don't talk on the ride to the apartment, probably because of the language barrier.

When the driver arrives at the apartment, I'm surprised to see a doorman. Then I remember, I never entered or exited through the front door the only day I was here. He opens my door and I step out, only to be photographed by three different people. They yell something in Italian and I just smile and wave. The doorman retrieves my luggage from the car and escorts me to the elevator and up to the penthouse. I'm met by a woman barely older than me. She greets me with a big hug and motions for me to follow her and the doorman to wait. She shows me the bedrooms and I select the one with the best view. Then we return to the doorman, who delivers my luggage to the room and receives a substantial tip.

I reach for one suitcase to bring unpacking, but the housekeeper, Maya, pats my arm and signals for me to follow her. She leads me to the kitchen where she has prepared a light lunch. While I eat, Maya disappears. I discover later; she unpacked my suitcases while I ate. Although many would consider me a wealthy woman, it would surprise them I do my laundry, cleaning, driving, and everything else I need done. I also need to communicate with Maya, so I download an app that translates as you talk to it. Bingo! Except I downloaded a Spanish app instead of an Italian app. Maya and I both laugh while I download the correct app.

CHAPTER 11

I use texts from Maya to keep up with Vi. I certainly don't want her to think I'm spying on her since she moved into the apartment. That might scare her away and make me really upset. I'm thrilled with Vi's choice in bedrooms, knowing how much she enjoyed the view from the living area. It seems Vi and Maya are getting along well, especially after Vi downloaded the correct translation app. I laughed hard at that.

Today is Friday. It's been a long week. Mateo, Antonio, and I have put many miles on the SUV we use for the foundation. I'm exhausted because a red-haired, blue-eyed siren invades my sleep each night, stirring up my feelings and my body as no one has before. I find myself napping on our drives between locations, whether it's five miles or fifty.

Mateo says we should be home by 11:00 pm. I hope so. I need to get some rest. Unfortunately, I have to attend the awards event tomorrow night. I'm presenting an award, not receiving one this time. Oh, and I have a date for the event with Marisol Montez, which I'm looking forward to. I've never worked with her but have been following her career. She may be a candidate for the new project we start filming in a couple of months. The director texted me and said he still hasn't selected a female lead for the TV show. I suggested Marisol, so we'll see what happens.

But most importantly, I think as I lie my head back against the cushions of the back seat, Vi is at the apartment. I can't wait to see and talk to her. The next thing I know, Mateo is shaking me awake and tells me we're home. I climb out of the SUV and go straight to my bed. Sleep doesn't come because I know the siren of my dreams is just a few feet away. After an hour of tossing and turning, I creep, yes creep, past Mateo's and Antonio's bedrooms to Vi's. She is lying on her side and I climb into bed next to her.

The sun shining in my face wakes me. I can tell it is high in the sky. The space beside me is empty. I get out of bed and make my way slowly to the closed door. I crack it and peer out. The other bedroom doors are closed and the smell of food waifs into my nostrils making me realize just how hungry I am. I walk into the kitchen to find Vi sitting at the breakfast table with a cup of coffee, admiring the view.

"Good morning, Vi," I say, rubbing my eyes.

"You mean, good afternoon sleepyhead. Did you sleep well?"

"I slept like a baby. Where is everyone?" I ask, looking around the room.

"Well, Mateo and Antonio left about an hour ago to pick up your tuxedo and check on the limo for tonight. They should be back soon. I gave Maya the morning off since she had the afternoon off anyway," Vi answers with a smile that could rival the sun.

"Do they know I slept in your room?" I ask tentatively.

"I don't see how," Vi says, getting up and pouring me a cup of coffee. "I was up early. Mateo wanted to check on you, but I told him to let you sleep."

"Thanks for that," I say, taking the offered cup of coffee. "What smells so good?"

"Mateo said they will serve no meal tonight, so I thought I would make all of you a hearty meal to get you through. It's a surprise and will be ready when they get back."

"That's very nice of you. Do I have time for a shower?" It is only when Vi's eyes travel the length of my body that I realize I'm standing in front of her in my boxers, with an enormous bulge that I would normally be proud of. "Uh, never mind," I reply as I refill my cup and head to my bedroom.

I hear voices when I open my bedroom door. Vi and Mateo are talking. Poor Mateo has to translate everything to Antonio in Spanish, so the conversation is short. The aroma of food fills the air.

"You're just in time," Vi says when she sees me. "Okay, everyone go sit in the dining room and I'll bring the food out." Antonio and I head to the table, but Mateo follows Vi to the kitchen, offering to help.

It only takes a few minutes for the table to be filled with food. Chicken fried steak, mashed potatoes, gravy, green beans, and a corn casserole fill the table. Everyone fills their plates and begins eating. I silently laugh as Antonio looks at the food curiously before Mateo tells him to dig in.

"Gentlemen, leave room for dessert," Vi says, smiling at the hearty appetites of three grown men.

"Vi, you have really gone to a great deal of trouble. I haven't had chicken fried steak in years. This tastes amazing," Mateo says.

"Mateo's right, Vi. I guess I should explain Mateo and I have been friends since I moved to Spain as a kid. He also went to

USC on a soccer scholarship and we graduated together. He returned to Spain when I did, so we've been together ever since," I tell her.

"And that's how I know about chicken fried steak," Mateo says with a chuckle and then repeats the conversation to Antonio.

Once we've had our fill, Vi stands and returns to the kitchen. When she comes back, she is carrying a steaming hot peach pie and homemade vanilla ice cream. We all moan because we ate too much food, but as a group of muscled up men, we never turn down dessert.

It is 4:00 pm by the time we finish eating. Mateo and Antonio leave to take a nap, and I stay to help Vi clean up even though she suggests perhaps I should nap as well. I stack the dirty plates and carry them to the kitchen, placing them on the counter while Vi carries in the glasses and sits them down beside me.

I take a step back, place my hands on her hips and turn her to face me, my nose a mere inch from hers. "Sweetheart, thank you. The meal was delicious. You're a splendid cook. That was so thoughtful of you to do," I whisper, moving my hands to cup her face.

"It was my pleasure. I need to earn my keep around here," Vi whispers back. We stare into each other's eyes as if searching for something for several seconds. Then, Vi says, "please don't tease me, Matt." She turns and walks back to the dining room, leaving me speechless.

We finish clearing the dining room table in silence, with me trying to make sense of her comment. I fail miserably.

"I'll finish up in here. You go lie down for a little while before you have to dress," Vi says, refusing to look at me.

"Okay," is all I can say. When I reach my bedroom door, I hear a small sob coming from the kitchen. My heart wants to go back and take Vi in my arms, but my mind won't let me.

CHAPTER 12

Dressed in my tux, I walk into the living area to find Vi curled on the sofa with a pen and notebook.

"Do you have an idea for your novel yet?" I ask.

"No, not yet," Vi answers and turns to look at me. She stands and walks over to me. "Wow! You are the reason women have wet dreams." Vi turns almost as red as her hair and says, "I'm so sorry. That kind of just slipped out." I can't help but laugh at the comment. "You look very handsome, Matt. May I straighten your tie?" I nod and she reaches up, careful not to touch my skin as she tugs on the tie.

When Vi's finished, she backs up and looks at me from top to bottom. "Matt, I know I don't ask questions, but I have to ask one now. What's with all the rings, necklaces, and everything else? You've never worn it around me?"

"That's a fair question, Vi. I've done two TV shows since **Ama el único camino**, but no one really remembers my character. They all want Enrique Salas, not Espíritu Libre. I don't know how to change that yet, so I give them what they want. It makes me, Matt, uncomfortable and I don't enjoy wearing all this stuff. With you, I don't feel the need to wear it because I can be my real self, not some character in a TV show. Does that make sense?"

"Yes, it does, and I truly understand better than most people, probably. I'm thrilled you are comfortable enough and trust me enough to be yourself." Then Vi does something that almost knocks me over. She places one hand on my bearded check and the other on my shoulder. Vi leans up and places a gentle kiss on my cheek. "I hope you have a good time tonight. I'll be watching it on TV," she whispers.

"We should go," Mateo announces, walking into the room with Antonio.

Vi quickly steps back and says, "my, don't the two of you look handsome," as she glances in their direction. "I know you're both working, so be careful and don't let any strange women attack your boss."

"No worries, Vi," Mateo says. "It's him we have to keep away from the women. He loves beautiful, well-endowed women. Let's go. We still need to pick up Ms. Montez."

I glance down at Vi's face. Is her expression one of hurt or disappointment? I wonder. I step forward and place a small kiss on her forehead. "Vi, I'll see you tomorrow," I say before turning to leave. When Mateo, Antonio, and I enter the elevator, I see Vi curled on the sofa with the TV remote in her hand and a sad look on her sweet face.

I wake up with a splitting headache and Marisol Montez naked in bed next to me. I remember the ceremony, and the after party, but that's it. The sexual tension that has built up over the last two weeks has passed, but I feel unsatisfied somehow. I watch as Marisol turns over, revealing everything that's fake about her body. My mind drifts to a woman with red hair, green eyes, and a 100% natural body. I shake my head to clear the cobwebs, which doesn't help my headache. I ease out of bed and walk to the bathroom where I swiftly down two ibuprofen and a glass of water. Then I head back to bed, hoping I feel better in a couple of hours.

CHAPTER 13

Since I stayed up late watching the awards show, I sleep until 9:00 am. While I shower, my mind drifts back to the red carpet scene before the show. Handsome, tuxedoed Matt being photographed with a blond beauty who probably paid more for her boob job than I have invested in the stock market. The woman is stunning. Well, now I know Matt's type and it definitely isn't an old woman like me, I decide.

After dressing, I open the door to find the apartment quiet, so I go into the kitchen and brew a pot of coffee. I realize I'm hungry and grab a croissant. Opening the fridge, I take out sliced cheese and some kind of sliced meat. While I'm sipping my first cup of coffee, I hear Matt's bedroom door open and the blond beauty from the red carpet walks out wrapped in a towel.

The woman eyes me up and down, scowls, and says something in Italian. When I don't respond, she pushes past me, grabs a cup off the counter and pours herself a cup of coffee. I ignore her and begin making my sandwich. Again, she says something I don't understand. When I finish the sandwich, I turn and place the unused cheese and meat back into the fridge. When I turn around, Ms. Blond Beauty grabs my sandwich and takes a bite while staring at me. Again, another verbal barrage in Italian. She rolls her eyes and lays my sandwich down on the plate. I pick up the plate, dump the sandwich in the trash, politely say "kiss my ass" in Italian and head for my bedroom. Then I grab my purse and as I press the call button for the elevator, I can hear Ms. Blond Beauty spewing Italian in a loud, rapid voice as Matt laughs uncontrollably. I can't help but smile. Of course, I learned all the bad Italian words first. Wouldn't you?

I walk five blocks to a small sidewalk café I noticed last week. Of course, they all speak very little English, so I pull out my phone. Between pointing at the menu and using the app, I finally order coffee, waffles, and bacon. They are busy and it takes a while to get my food, but I'm not in a hurry. I take out my journal and make notes as I watch people enter and exit the café. I'm just about to stick my first bite of waffle in my mouth when my phone pings next to my plate. It is Matt texting me.

"Where are you?"

My first inclination is to ignore him, so I take a couple of bites and then answer.

"Having breakfast."

"Okay. Where?"

"I don't know where." I reply.

"Take a picture and send it to me."

"Why?"

"I'm hungry."

I laugh aloud at the text. After I take a couple more bites, I text him back. "Hard to believe."

"Don't be a smartass. Send me a picture." So what does stupid me do? I send him a picture. Ugh!

"Be there in a few minutes. Don't leave!!!!!" Then another text comes in. "Take your phone to the counter, ask for Pierre, dial my number and then give him the phone."

"Of course, your highness. Anything else I can do for you? PS—if you bring that crazy woman, I'm moving out today even if I have to go home." I smile but wait. Matt surely wouldn't be stupid enough to bring her. Would he? I get up and follow his royal highness' instructions. Pierre smiles as he talks to Matt on the phone. Then he hangs up, talks to another man, and waves for me to follow him.

I follow Pierre to a table in the café's rear that is partially hidden by a curtain. He pulls a chair out and motions for me to sit down. I point toward my table and food. Pierre leaves, gathers everything but my food, and brings it to me. When I look up at him in confusion, he smiles and holds up his index finger before leaving.

"Boy, my day just keeps getting better and better," I say aloud.

"Does it?" Matt's deep voice says as he slides into the chair across from me. I roll my eyes at him in frustration. Pierre arrives at that moment with fresh coffee for both of us and returns a minute later with Matt's food and a fresh plate of my order.

"I see you came alone," I say with a smirk.

"I seriously doubt Marisol would have come if I had told her I was meeting you," Matt says returning my smirk.

"What was her deal, anyway?"

"She thought you were the housekeeper. She didn't approve of your clothing choice, nor the fact that you didn't get her a cup of coffee. I have to say throwing the sandwich in the trash after she took a bite and then telling her to kiss your ass was hilarious. I wish I could have seen it." Matt smiles as he takes a sip of his coffee.

"She shouldn't have taken a bite of my sandwich," I state, and we both burst out laughing.

Matt takes a bite of his waffle and asks, "what are your plans for today, sweetheart?"

"I haven't decided yet and please stop calling me that."

"I'm sorry. Does it offend you?" he asks quietly, studying my face.

"No, but it's typically a term of endearment between two people who care deeply about one another," I answer.

"Oh, I see." Matt looks down at his plate. We eat for several minutes in silence. Then he says, "if you like, I can take you to a couple of those neighborhoods today if you haven't already been."

"I can find them on my own. You'll probably be ready for a nap after you finish your meal," I retort.

"Vi, look at me." I see something in Matt's eyes. Is it hurt or disgust? I wonder. "I want to spend the rest of the day with you because I've missed you very much."

I look at his man bun and sunglasses. "We will not get very far with you looking like that."

Matt looks down at his black T-shirt. "Yeah, I guess you're right about that."

"I have an idea. Stay here. I'll be right back." I stand up.

"What about your food?"

"I had already eaten half my order before I had to take my phone to Pierre. That's really weird, you know. A guy with a French name in an Italian county, and you talk to him in Spanish." That brings a smile to Matt's serious face. "What size shirt do you wear?"

"2X or XX. Why?" I smile and leave Matt wondered what I'm doing.

I walk across the street to a souvenir shop I found last week. I pick up a few items quickly and return to Matt, who has finished his meal. As I sit down, I reach into the bag. "Here," I say as I had him a 3X jersey with an American pro football team logo. Next, I hand him a baseball cap with the same logo. While he pulls the jersey over his head, I slip a matching smaller one over my head. I pull my hair into a ponytail and put my cap on.

"Now, we look like American tourists," I say as I slide a pair of obnoxious sunglasses on.

"Vi, you never cease to amaze me," Matt says with a huge smile.

"Now, I'll do the talking if we're stopped. You pretend you have a sore throat, laryngitis or something, and only whisper in my ear if you need to tell me something. Ready to go?"

Matt stands and offers me his hand. "I'm as ready as I'll ever be. Let's get out of here." He grabs my back pack and throws it over his shoulder. "Dang, woman, what do you have in here?"

"Just a few things I thought I might need today," I answer with a smile. Matt waves at Pierre as we step away from the table and walk into the busy Rome street.

CHAPTER 14

I stop Vi on the sidewalk in front of the café. "If we are going to do charade, we should really work it," I tell her.

"What do you have in mind?" she asks. I can see the curiosity in her eyes.

"I think we should pretend to be on a honeymoon, or at least be lovers. I am a highly paid actor, you know," I answer with a big smile.

"Whatever," Vi says, rolling her eyes. I toss the backpack over my other shoulder, pull Vi closer, and put my arm around her neck, leading her down the street. We don't travel three blocks before three women stop us. In Italian, one asks if I'm Espíritu Libre.

Vi puts on a confused expression and says, "English?" The woman nods and asks again in English.

Vi looks at me and states, "we don't know who that is. We're from the US and just got married." I pull Vi closer and look down at her as the woman looks up at me. "My husband has a cold and lost his voice," Vi says, rubbing her throat. At that moment, I fake two consecutive sneezes and give a small smile. The woman apologizes, and she and the other two women walk past us.

I lean over and whisper, "great acting, Vi. We're supposed to begin filming a new show in a couple of months and still need a female lead. Are you available?" Vi rolls her eyes and elbows me in the side. I wink at her and we walk another block.

Suddenly, Vi's phone pings with a message. She ignores it, but two more pings happen in rapid succession. "Sorry, I meant to mute it," she says. "I better read the text since there are so many." I remove my arm from her shoulders and step back, giving Vi her privacy. "Oh, wow!" she says in an excited voice.

"Is everything okay?" I ask in a voice low enough that only she can hear.

"It's my assistant. My book just hit #1 on the bestseller list."

"Congratulations. That's wonderful news. We should celebrate," I say.

"I like that idea. What do you suggest?"

"Well, there's a black tie fundraiser Saturday night. I bought two tickets but hadn't planned to go. It's just a few speeches, dinner, and dancing afterwards."

"Oh, Matt. That sound like fun."

"You'll need a dress."

"Wait, I bought one before I left for an awards ceremony in New York in a couple of weeks. I'll have my assistant ship it here." Vi begins tapping out a text message to her assistant while I wait. When she finished, she looks past me. "Matt, those three women are following us. I guess we weren't as convincing as I thought."

"How close are they?" I whisper.

"About half a block away," Vi replies.

I look around the street and then say, "okay. Let them get a little closer and then say now." Vi nods and we pretend to point at different shops along the street.

"Now," Vi says.

I grab her wrist and pull her into an alleyway next to where we were standing. I watch for the women over my shoulder, and when they approach the entrance to the alley, I push Vi against the wall, blocking her in with both hands. Then I kiss her. The kiss is not hard, but it's not soft either. At the touch of her perfect lips to mine, my blood heats quickly, and I want to kiss her more. I hear one woman say something in Italian and watch them walk away out of the corner of my eye. I lean back just enough for the tip of my nose to touch Vi's and look into her eyes. Her blue eyes are soft and dreamy.

"That wasn't your typical TV show kiss," Vi whispers.

"It wasn't supposed to be," I reply.

"What did the woman say before they left?"

"It's not important," I answer.

"Matt, please tell me. I'm a big girl."

Still looking into those beautiful blue eyes, I say, "she said I couldn't be Espíritu Libre because he wouldn't kiss an older woman." There is a flash of hurt in Vi's eyes before she looks down and tries to escape my hands, but I don't move. I move one hand to lift her chin so she has to look at me. "One day soon, I'm going to prove her wrong. I'm going to kiss an older woman and I am going to enjoy it so much my eyes, my lips, and my body are going to beg for more. She will enjoy it just as much and will beg for more, too."

"Oh," Vi says. "You said you were going to film soon." She places her hands on my chest and pushes me backwards so she can move away.

I rub my hands over my face in frustration. Dammit, Vi didn't understand that I meant her. I will just have to find the perfect time and show her. When I turn, Vi is standing on the sidewalk waiting for me. I take her hand even though she doesn't look at me and we continue walking down the street.

Since we are getting closer to neighborhoods, the streets are quieter and you can hear children playing in the park. The only people we meet are families pushing strollers and older people. We walk one mile and then turn a corner. Vi's eyes light up as she recognizes the street from the TV show.

"Oh Matt, this is beautiful. Will your new show be on streets like this?" she asks.

"I'm not sure. It's a good script, but the producer is talking about a location in Sicily." Vi releases my hand and grabs my bicep as we walk the entire length of the street when she spots an open market.

"Let's go inside," she says, "but first, I need to get something out of the backpack." I pull the backpack off my shoulder and hand it to her. She takes out a bag and then returns the backpack to me. After I fling it over my shoulder, Vi grabs my hand and practically drags me into the market.

CHAPTER 15

Oh my gosh, this is exactly what I was hoping to find this afternoon. Only now, I have to buy enough for two people instead of one. I drag Matt behind me. My first stop is a small stall where I buy a small loaf of bread. The next stall sells various kinds of cheese where I buy two different types. Several stalls down the aisle, I find a vendor selling fruit. I buy two large apples, a dozen chocolate-covered strawberries, half dark chocolate and half white chocolate. The last stop sells coffee. I buy two cups and two bottles of water. Poor Matt has followed me around without saying a word and now gentlemanly takes the full bag from my hand.

"Where to, madam?" he leans close and whispers in my ear. Suggesting Matt pretend to have laryngitis was a stupid idea because every time he breathes into my ear, his warm breath sends a heat wave over my entire body.

"We need a park," I say, trying to bring my feelings under control. The look in Matt's eyes tells me I am failing miserably.

"Follow me," he says with a tender look. At the end of the block, we turn the corner and walk two more blocks. A small neighborhood park is directly in front of us and it's empty.

I lead Matt to a large tree. "Here," I say, pointing to the ground. He grins and sets the backpack and bag on the ground. I unzip the backpack and pull out a light blanket. Matt helps me spread it out and then I sit down, patting the space beside me. He has a curious look on his face. As he sits down, he says nothing, but watches what I do.

Reaching into the backpack, I pull out two napkins. Inside one napkin are two knives. I lay both napkins on the blanket between us. Out of the bag, I pull all the food I purchased and set it on the napkins. I hand Matt his coffee and set mine on the other side of me.

Matt places one of his large hands on my bare knee. "Woman, you are the goddess of organization. I'm impressed." I look at him and his eyes shine with a brightness that unnerves me.

"Here," I say, handing him one knife. "You slice the bread." Matt slices the bread while I use the other knife to cube the cheeses and slice the apples.

We enjoy a nice leisurely lunch and talk about the park and the neighborhood. Matt tells me he discovered the park one day at lunch break from filming. It was his place to get away and have quiet time.

"Can I lay my head in your lap?" Matt asks when we're finished.

"Sure. Let me lean back against the tree and I'll feed you strawberries," I answer as I scoot backwards. Matt lies down and puts his head in my lap. I open the bag of strawberries. "Do you prefer the white or the dark?"

"Both, please." First, I feed him a dark one and then I eat one. Next, we both eat a white one. It is warm outside, and the chocolate is getting soft. When I feed him the next dark one, my fingers are covered in chocolate. I watch as Matt pulls my hand to his mouth and sucks the chocolate off my fingers. I nearly pass out. How can something so simple turn me on so much? I wonder. I'm going to have a heat stroke and melt into the blanket. So I have to look away and pray Matt doesn't notice my shortness of breath.

"Vi, why did you get a divorce?" Such a simple question with a complicated answer.

I breathe deeply. "He cheated on me." I didn't elaborate that he cheated with a younger woman even though I was twenty-nine.

"Did you have any children?" Matt asks innocently. Ugh! Another simple question with a complicated answer.

"We tried, but it didn't work out."

"What about with your second husband?"

Where are these questions coming from? Is he trying to hurt me? Is this some type of punishment for the fact he turns me inside out and he knows it? "My second husband was slightly older than me and he already had two kids."

Finally, Matt is quiet, and I take a deep breath. I look down at him and he's sleeping. Well, why not? He was up all night with Ms. Big Boobs, that thought I was the maid. I sigh and lay by head back against the tree. I made a conscience decision to limit my touching him after our first dance. Now I can't resist. I take his cap off and run my hand over the top of his head softly so I don't wake him. As Matt's breathing slows, I gently touch his full beard and suddenly I realize what I've feared the most. Millions of people all over Europe have fallen in love with Espíritu Libre, but I'm falling for Matthew Carson.

CHAPTER 16

I feel Vi's tender touch on my hair and beard and wonder what she's thinking. She rarely touches me, but when she does, fireworks explode in my body and unexplained feelings surface.

When I can't take it anymore, I open my eyes and look directly into hers. "Vi, what are you doing?" I ask.

Her perfect, pink lips form a smirk and she replies, "admiring the view." That makes me grin. "Oh, wait. You trimmed your mustache. I can actually see all of your lips."

"I did it just for you."

"I doubt that. You did it for Ms. Big Boobs."

I can't help but chuckle. Do I hear a hint of jealousy? I wonder. "No, sweetheart. I trimmed it just before I met you at the café," I reply and close my eyes again. She asked me not to call her that and she is probably frowning right now.

I must have dozed off because large drops of water on my calves wake me. I open my eyes to find Vi holding an umbrella over me with one hand and cramming our picnic items and her purse in the backpack with the other. Then the sky opens up, and a downpour begins.

"I better call Mateo and tell him to pick us up," I say while Vi nods and keeps shoving things into the backpack.

"My backpack is waterproof, so put your phone in here when you finish," she says.

I call Mateo and tell him where we are and to bring plenty of towels. Then I hang up and look at Vi. "He said he would be here in twenty minutes. Are you okay?" She nods, giggles her cute little merry sound, and hands me the umbrella. Vi jumps up and runs out from under the tree to stand in the downpour. I watch for a few seconds and it feels like a bolt of lightning strikes me because I lose my breath and my heart beats uncontrollably. This beautiful, red-haired siren has touched my mind, my heart, and my soul. I am falling in love with her.

"Come dance with me," Vi yells over the rain. I smile, close the umbrella, and join her. We dance to a melody only each of us can hear, like two crazy children. Then I grab her, pulling her into my arms. I hum my favorite song and we slowly dance for a long time.

A honking car breaks the spell and I see Mateo with the car at the curb about twenty feet away. I wave for him to stay in the car. Vi and I rush to gather our things and then run to the car. Mateo opens the trunk automatically and I throw our things in while Vi climbs into the back seat. I climb in beside Mateo, who rolls his eyes at me.

"I brought plenty of towels and two robes so the two of you don't get sick," Mateo says, pointing to the back seat and then turning up the heat in the car.

"Vi, hand me a couple of towels. You slip on a robe quickly," I tell her. After handing me the towels, she wraps one towel around her head and turns her back to the front seat. I face forward and turn the rear-view mirror up to give her privacy. A few minutes later, Vi hands me the other robe and I quickly shuck my clothes for the warmth of the robe.

We ride in silence to the apartment. Once we arrive in the underground parking area, Vi and I get out. Mateo says he will take care of the wet clothes, our items, and the now wet interior of the car.

"Are you cold?" I ask as we enter the elevator.

"No, I'm good," Vi replies. "Are you?"

"Nope, but I think you're insane."

"I probably am, but it sure was fun."

"Yes, Vi. It was a lot of fun," I say as the elevator door opens and we walk inside my apartment. "I'll put on a pot of coffee. Let's change, and I'll meet you in the kitchen." Vi gives me a smile and hurries off toward her bedroom.

It doesn't take long for me to shed the robe, dry off, and slip on a pair of shorts, so I beat Vi to the kitchen. When she walks in wearing a T-shirt and capris, her wet hair hangs below her shoulders and I can see the waves forming. I offer her a cup of coffee.

"Are you hungry? I thought we could order in."

"I am starved, but I guess I should admit that I hate fish, cucumbers, melons, and I refuse to eat meat from baby animals," Vi says.

"Good to know. I'll order pizza." I look around and she laughs. "What?" I ask.

"Our phones are in the backpack. Do you plan on yelling at the pizza place?"

Without thinking, I rush over to her and begin tickling her. "You think that's funny?" Vi laughs and struggles slightly, trying to get away, but I hold her steady. Her laughter is contagious and I finally have to release her because my stomach hurts from laughing myself. Instantly, my arms ache to hold her again. I shake my head and walk into the living area where the landline phone sits on a table in the corner.

"A landline. How old school," Vi says, having followed me into the room.

"The security and alarm system are tied to a landline in the event of an emergency. It's a requirement," I answer. Then I dial the phone and place our pizza order. When I finish, I take Vi's hand in mine. "I have some place to go tomorrow and I'd like you to go. It's important to me to have you with me."

Vi looks up at me with innocent eyes. "Okay. What time do we leave and what should I wear?"

I feel excited that she's agreed to go. "I think a blouse and skirt would be appropriate." She nods, removes her hand from mine, and goes into her bedroom.

"She's good for you," Mateo says, walking into the room.

"You mean she's too good for me, Mateo?"

"No, that's not what I said. You're a different person when she's around. You're like my old friend, Matt Carson, before all this crazy TV star stuff started. And you are also falling for her. Falling hard and fast."

I study Mateo and then ask, "am I that obvious?"

"To me you are. I see it in the way you look at her," he replies.

"Do you think she sees it?"

"I don't know. You're the one that suggested the two of you be friends. I have seen nothing from her actions that would make me think otherwise."

I sigh. "It was a stupid idea on my part."

"I guess you'll just have to change her mind if you're serious. Did you order something?" Mateo asks as the buzzer downstair goes off.

"Yeah, enough pizza for an army."

The following day, Vi and I sit in the backseat, while Mateo and Antonio sit in the front. It is a thirty-minute drive to our destination, allowing me ample time to look at Vi from the corner of my eye. She is dressed in a black pencil skirt that hits just above her knees when she stands and rides up her thighs as she sits quietly beside me. Her blouse is a silky blue that brings out the color of her eyes. Last, black three-inch heels cover her feet. She looks amazing.

My phone pings with an incoming call. I look at the screen and ignore it. Vi looks at me curiously, so I lean over and whisper that I need to take it in private later.

Confusion covers Vi's face when we pull up to a vacant warehouse. As I help her out of the car, the skirt rides up even farther, showing off more of her creamy thighs. My body reacts below my waist and I'm thankful I didn't tuck my shirt in. I lead her through a door, waiting to see her reaction once we are inside.

Vi's eyes fill with wonder as she looks around the building. There are many workers and the construction sounds are loud, but wonderful to my ears. The foreperson approaches the four of us, handing out hard hats and ear plugs with a huge smile. We talk in Italian for a few minutes, and I watch Vi take in her surroundings.

Once the foreperson leaves, I remove one ear plug from Vi's soft ear and whisper. "This is my dream of a residence home for Alzheimer's and dementia patients who have no other place to go. There will be individual rooms with separate bathrooms and sitting areas. The courtyard in the middle will be a tiny park where they can get fresh air and sunshine. The staff, kitchen, and medical facilities will be on the top floor."

Vi turns her head toward me with tears filling her eyes. "It's fantastic," she says as a few tears begin running down her cheeks. I brush the tears away before handing her my handkerchief. I place the ear plug back in her ear and take her hand, heading toward the elevator. Mateo follows. It is a brief ride and I give Vi a tour of the top floor, which is two-thirds finished. Her smile warms my heart as we walk through each area.

Back downstairs, I show her the architectural drawings of the patients' rooms and a common dining area. As we talk, a friend and investor approaches.

"Spirit," he shouts over the noise. I wave and we all go outside to talk in quieter surroundings.

"Enzo, what a surprise," I say, shaking his hand. "This is my friend ..."

"Ivy Webber," Enzo says.

"I'm sorry. Have we met before?" Vi asks.

Enzo laughs, takes Vi's hand, and kisses her hand. "No, we've never met, but my wife's read all your books, so I recognize you from your photos. She's been after me to turn one into a movie, but she can't decide which one."

"Vi, I mean Ivy, meet Enzo Romano, an investor in the foundation and successful Italian movie producer."

Enzo, Vi and I talk for several minutes about the project and then Enzo leaves. I tell Mateo and Antonio to wait in the car while Vi and I walk around the building. Once we are around the corner, I take my phone out of my pocket and listen to the voice mail. I then send several texts messages and receive several in return. Vi watches me with concern on her face. When I slide the phone back into my pocket, she asks if Mateo should take her back to the apartment so I can tend to business.

"No, that was Mateo's mother. Tomorrow is his birthday and his mother and father are coming to surprise him."

"Well, that sounds like a party is needed." Vi's face lights up.

"Whoa! Hold on, girl. I have to be in Latina tomorrow for a book signing and then have an investor meeting in Rome in the afternoon."

"You go. I'll take care of everything."

"Says the goddess of organization." I laugh, which makes Vi's perfect lips smirk in response. "I'll leave Antonio with you. He can pick up Mateo's parents at the airport."

"Does Antonio know them?"

"Antonio is Mateo's nephew, so I should hope so."

Vi rolls her eyes. "You could have told me that sooner, you know. Great! Between Antonio, Maya, and me, everything will be a surprise. That is, if you can keep a secret," Vi says.

"Oh sweetheart, I'm very good at keeping secrets." She doesn't comment about the sweetheart, but I think it's because she's excited to plan a party. "There's one other thing I should tell you. Mateo's father suffered a stroke a couple of years ago. I let them stay in my bedroom because it is easier for them. I'll need to move some things into the bedroom next to you."

"It will be obvious if you move them. If you can lie out what you need before you leave in the morning, I'll move it for you," Vi states. "This will be so much fun. I haven't planned a birthday party in years. What kind of cake does Mateo like?"

I can't help but roll my eyes at her enthusiasm. "Italian Crème. I've seen him eat an entire cake in one sitting. Now, let's go have lunch." I place my hand at the small of her back and lead her to the car. As I get in, I look at Antonio and think, I'm sorry, I'm leaving you with a whirlwind tomorrow.

CHAPTER 17

I don't know what Matt told Antonio to make him stay, but he smiles at me after Mateo and Matt leave at 8:00 am. Well, this should be interesting. Maya speaks Italian, Antonio Spanish, and I, well, I struggle with English. LOL Fortunately, Mateo's parents don't arrive until 1:00 pm.

I need party favors, and a banner, so I show Antonio pictures off the internet. Luckily, he understands because I promised Matt that I would try not to bug him with phone calls or text messages. Once Antonio leaves, Maya and I move everything Matt laid out on the bed to the bedroom next to mine. Using my translation app, Maya explains this is common when Mateo's parents visit.

Next on the agenda, I need to make out a list of food items to buy. I decide I would make my version of lasagna, and of course, Italian Crème Cake. Maya has made the cake before, thank goodness, because that would be a new one for me. I invite Maya to stay for dinner, but she refuses.

While Maya and I wait for Antonio to return, I text Matt.

"Oh mighty, skilled, and talented chef! I need help."

"Yes, wench?" I laugh aloud.

"I need a food store that sells American food products if possible."

"Dante's is best. Antonio knows where it is. What are you up to?"

"I'm busy. Don't eat a large lunch and don't return before 4:00."

"Okay, but you should know that I'm mighty, skilled, and talented in other things as well."

"Maybe you could show me some of your other talents one day."

"It's already on the agenda for the future, winking emoji."

I don't have time to wonder what he means because Antonio walks in the door with the goodies. He places the bags on the kitchen island. Maya and I pull everything out of the bags to inspect the items. Antonio did perfect and bought more party items than I sent him for. He also picked out the perfect wrapping paper and bow for my gift to Mateo. I hug him tightly and tell him thanks in Spanish. Now, off to the food store.

Matt's suggested food store is perfect. I find everything I need as poor Antonio pushes the heavy cart behind Maya and me. The only problem I run into is when I reach for familiar jars of spaghetti sauce. Maya picks up the lasagna noodles from the cart and shakes her head and finger at me in disgust. Now we have to backtrack through the store so she can get items for homemade sauce.

While Antonio heads to the airport and Maya works on the cake and sauce, I wrap my gift. The box of first edition books my assistant sent was delivered this morning. I autograph each one with a different message and then wrap the box. Next, I decorate the dining room. I'm almost finished when Antonio and Mateo's parents arrive. Matt said the older couple speaks excellent English, so we have a pleasant chat before the two lie down for a nap.

"On our way. I hope you're ready. We skipped lunch."

"Ready says the organization goddess. Curious about your other talents."

"One day very soon," is Matt's last text.

Mateo's parents and Antonio hide in the living area. Maya has left for the day and the lasagna is almost done when Matt and Mateo walk in. I've closed the dining room door so the decorations can't be seen with the gifts sitting on a table to the side. Earlier, Antonio brought in gifts from Matt and himself that he had hidden in his bedroom, as well as Mateo's parents' gift, while I struggled to carry mine in.

"It smells heavenly in here," Matt says, stepping off the elevator.

"Now I'm glad you insisted on skipping lunch," Mateo says.

"Who said I invited you to dinner?" Matt asks, punching him in the shoulder.

"Well, it's about time you got here," I state. "Wash up and go sit in the living area while I get everything on the table and no, I don't need any help."

I'm busy taking the salad and homemade vinaigrette to the dining room when I hear laughter and happy squeals from the living area. I smile. Next, I take the bubbling lasagna from the oven and place it on the table. I know those big guys are hungry, but I hope they don't eat it all. I promised Maya I would save her some.

"We are ready to eat now," I say, walking to the entrance of the living area. Everyone rises and follows me to the dining room. When I open the door, I glance over my shoulder and see a very surprised Mateo stop and stare at all the decorations. His mother hugs him tightly, bringing tears to my eyes.

Everyone sits down. Matt sits at the head of the table while Mateo sits between his parents. Antonio sits across from Mateo, leaving the chair next to Matt vacant. But, I don't sit down. I stand beside the table serving heaping chunks of lasagna while the salad and dressing are being passed around and the wine flows freely.

After I refill the wine glasses, I retreat to the kitchen, where I place the special candle Antonio bought on the cake. The laughter and loud voices coming from the dining room make my heart ache. It's moments like this that make me miss my parents so much. They always made my birthday special, no matter how old I was.

I turn my back to the doorway and wipe the tears from my cheeks. Then large, strong arms wrap around me from behind. I don't turn around because I don't want Matt to see my tears.

"Aren't you going to eat?" he asks.

"No, I've got a couple of things to do first. Is everyone almost finished eating?"

"Yes, do you need any help?" I shake my head no and he returns to the dining room.

I dry my tears and light the candle on the cake. Then I carry it into the dining room, trying to be careful because the candle Antonio bought is like a 4th of July sparkler. Everyone sings some Spanish song I assume is their version of Happy Birthday, as Mateo grins like a four-year-old. I feel Matt's eyes on me as I return to the kitchen. I can feel the love from the dining room. Matt told me Mateo's parents were like a second set of parents to him. I smile weakly. My heart still aches.

Matt and Antonio bring in the dirty china and crystal soon after and set them on the counter. I return to the dining room, thankful to see one helping of lasagna remains for Maya. Once the table is cleared, Matt insists on Mateo opening his gifts. I watch from the doorway.

Mateo's parents' gift is a beautiful blue suit. Matt's gift is a pair of diamond studded cuff links. Antonio's gift, well, his gift, is an obnoxious T-shirt. Matt sits my heavy gift on the table in front of Mateo. I deliberately did not put a tag or card on it, announcing it was from me. Mateo looks around the room and everyone just shrugs.

The wrapping is shredded, and the bow is history by the time Mateo opens the box. He removes the first book, which is the newest one, reads the inscription, and looks at me with tears in his eyes. Of course, this gesture brings tears to mine. Mateo stands, walks over to me, places his huge, inked arms around me, and hugs me so tightly I can barely breathe. No words pass between us because they aren't needed. When he lets go, I usher everyone into the living area so I can finish cleaning up. I refuse to leave anything for Maya.

When I finish, I go straight to my room, bypassing all the laughter. I sit on my bed and the tears flow hard and fast. I lie on my bed sobbing into my pillow.

CHAPTER 18

I head to the kitchen, expecting to see Vi cleaning up. I know her well enough that she won't leave a mess for Maya to clean tomorrow. The kitchen is empty and silent except for the dishwasher. I walk down the hall toward her bedroom and find the door closed.

I start to knock on the door and invite her to join us, but I hear a faint sob. So I ease the door open and find Vi lying on her stomach, sobbing into her pillow. Pulling my shoes off as I go, I lie down beside her and pull her into my arms. She comes with no hesitation. I lie her head on my shoulder and let her cry. The sobs are hard and break my heart, but I grip her. After a while, the sobs turn into hiccups. Then Vi lies her head on my chest, falling asleep instantly.

The alarm from my phone wakes Vi. I've been awake several minutes watching her sleep. Her red hair splayed out across my chest and stomach.

"Good morning, sweetheart," I whisper when she raises her head to look at me. She blushes the bright pink color.

"Uh, good morning. Did I sleep on you all night?"

"Maybe. I'm not sure. I fell asleep too."

"Thank you, Matt," Vi murmurs, not meeting my eyes.

Not wanting to embarrass her any further, I say, "ok, Vi. It's time to get up, shower, dress, and pack an overnight bag for two nights."

"Why?" she asks, rising on her elbow.

"You're coming with me. I gave Mateo today and tomorrow off to spend with his parents. They need some time alone."

"Okay. What should I pack?"

I smile softly, looking into her swollen, red eyes. "Casual clothes are fine. Whatever you're comfortable in. I have book signings and nightclubs to visit. You can shower first because I need to pack." I untangle Vi from my body and climb off the bed, going through the shared bathroom to my temporary bedroom.

One and a half hours later, Vi and I sit in the back seat while Antonio drives.

"I'm sorry about last night," Vi says in a low voice.

"Do you want to talk about it?"

"I just missed my parents so much. Birthdays were always special occasions at our house. Besides, sometimes women just need a good cry." Vi's voice is barely a whisper on the last statement.

Grasping her hand in mine, I reach over to lift her chin so she looks at me. "Promise me that whenever you need to cry, you let me know so I can hold you. It's one of my talents."

This brings a small smile to her face, and she asks, "had much practice?"

"The divorce was hard on my mom. That's all," I answer as heartbreaking memories of holding my mother as she cried over the divorce entering my mind. I clear my throat before continuing. "Will you promise me that, Vi?" She nods and our eyes lock. Each of us searching. I don't know what Vi is searching for, but I'm searching for something more than friendship. We stay that way for several minutes before Vi looks away. I continue to hold her hand as we travel the rest of the way to Palermo.

We stop for lunch when we reach the city. Next, we head to a downtown bookstore where one hundred people wait to see Espíritu Libre. I smile, autograph books, and take selfies, all the while keeping my eyes on Vi. She sits quietly at the back of the store, watching me. When I finish, I speak to Antonio. He leaves my side and takes Vi to the car. Then he returns to me where he and several police escort me through the crowd to the car. Cameras flash as I get in beside Vi, who is leaning over, hiding her face.

I wave to the crowd as we leave and then turn to Vi. "You don't have to hide."

"I don't want to ruin your reputation," she replies with a smirk.

"Sorry, sweetheart, but I am proud to be seen with you. Reputation be damned." I mean it. I've been photographed with some of the most gorgeous women in Europe. None of them can compare to the woman beside me who is holding my heart in her hands without knowing it.

After checking into the hotel, Vi and I arrive at my room. "I forgot to mention that the reservation was made weeks ago and there's only one bed," I say with a smirk.

"That's getting to be a habit with you," she replies with a grin.

"Guilty," I say, walking over to the balcony opening the doors. "Hey, come look at this view." Vi walks beside me and sits in one chair. "Do you mind if I take a nap?" I ask.

"No, go ahead. I doubt you got much sleep last night holding this crybaby."

"I'll hold you forever if you'll let me," quietly, slips out of my mouth before I realize it. Quickly, I turn and head for the bed, wondering if Vi heard me. If she did, she never mentions it. My phone pings with a message from Mateo as I lie down. A package has arrived for Vi. I bet it's her dress. I tell Mateo to open the package. If it is the dress, have it pressed and make an appointment for a spa afternoon for Vi before our night out at the fundraiser.

The next days pass by quickly. I'm busy meeting fans, and Vi is with me every step of the way. She always sits at the very back of the room, watching me with a smile on her face and a distant look in her eyes.

We arrive back at the apartment late Friday night. Mateo's parents have left, and he moved all my items back to my bedroom. Vi heads to her bedroom and I go to mine. But after sleeping in the same bed with Vi the past two nights, I have trouble falling asleep. Yes, our sleeping arrangements were innocent, but I loved waking up every morning with her in my arms. How that happened, I have no idea.

We sleep in and after lunch, Mateo whisks Vi off for her spa treatment. She was pleased to find Mateo had taken care of her dress and surprised by the spa afternoon. I didn't see the dress beforehand, and I knew I wouldn't see Vi until we were ready to leave for the fundraiser. I have to admit; the anticipation was killing me. I heard her when she returned and was tempted to sneak a peek, but I showered, trimmed my beard, and dressed in my tux. Tonight I would be myself, not playing the part of Espíritu Libre, so all the jewelry stays home.

I anxiously wait in the living area for Vi. Mateo sits on the sofa, smiling. Lucky dog got to see her when he picked her up and brought her back. He's also seen the dress. I pace the room, nervous as a cat in a room full of rocking chairs. I heard that expression in a movie a long time ago. LOL!

Mateo clears his throat and I stop pacing to look up. Standing in the doorway is the most gorgeous woman I have ever seen. They piled her red mane up on top of her head, revealing her sculpted neck. Her dress is candy apple red. (Okay, I'll explain it as best I can.) It is an off the shoulder evening gown. The dress is fitted to enhance Vi's perfect curves. The front dips down, revealing cleavage I would love to kiss. Slits on each side of the bottom show off her thighs. Black sandals show Vi's red toenails. HOT DAMN!!!!!!!!

"Matt, the car is ready downstairs," I hear Mateo say, but he must be in a tunnel because his voice sounds far away.

"Cancel it," I say, moving my eyes up over the goddess before me.

"Why?" Mateo asks.

"Because we're staying in so I can look at this beautiful woman all night," I answer when my eyes finally meet hers.

Vi giggles. "I didn't get all dressed up to stay home, Matt. Either we go or I change." Her eyes sparkle as she stares into mine.

"Okay, but we can't go yet. Something is missing." I reach into my pocket for the velvet-covered box Mateo had left on my bed while I was showering. I walk to Vi and open the box, revealing a stunning sapphire necklace with matching earrings.

Vi inhales sharply when she sees the contents of the box. "Matt, this is beautiful."

"They match your eyes. May I put your necklace on?" She nods. While I remove the necklace from the box, Vi turns around. I almost pass out when I look up. The back of the dress is open to her butt. I don't know what kind of sound I make, but Vi asks if I'm okay and I struggle to get the word yes out. I reach around to place the jewel encrusted necklace around her neck. A new fragrance hits my nose. She smells wonderful. I take my time fastening the necklace so I can touch Vi's creamy silk. "There." I step back. "You better put the earrings in." I receive another giggle.

"Are you sure I look okay?" Vi asks as she turns around to face me when the earrings are in place.

I touch her cheek. "Sweetheart, I'll kill any man that touches you anywhere except for your hand." Mateo clears his throat. "We better go, if we're going," I say.

Vi takes my arm and leans into me. "You look edible tonight, Mr. Carson." I damn near melt into a puddle in the middle of my apartment.

CHAPTER 19

"Wow! This must be a big deal," Vi says as we pull into the driveway and wait our turn at the valet station.

"It is bigger than the Italian Oscars. It's Enzo's event. All the money goes to his favorite charities across Italy. Fortunately, my foundation is one he favors."

When we finally exit the limo, cameras flash all around us, blinding me. Matt whispers not to look directly at the photographers, just smile. We walk up a red carpet to the entrance with Mateo and Antonio behind us. Once inside, I notice various couples being photographed and interviewed.

One man waves at Matt, and we head in his direction. He leads us to a backdrop of white and begins taking pictures as another man joins him and asks questions in Italian. I assume he asks my name because Matt replies, Ivy. Matt whispers in my ear that the man wants to know who my dress designer is. I giggle and tell him it's me.

Suddenly, we are overwhelmed with photographers. Matt turns us at different angles for various photographs while answering questions. His possessive hands never leave my hips or back. Finally, we get to leave all the hoopla and walk into a massive tent filled with tables and twinkling lights. Thank goodness, because my feet are killing me by now.

"Spirit!" a loud voice says over the conversations taking place all around us.

Matt turns us in man's direction. "Enzo," he says as he takes the man's hand.

"Ivy, you look stunning," Enzo says, and he kisses both my cheeks. As I thank him, a petite woman steps beside him. "Ivy Webber, meet your biggest fan, my wife Sophia."

"Ivy, so nice to meet you. Enzo said he met you the other day at the warehouse. I love your books and I got the latest one mid-week but haven't started it. I have a book club and we read all your books. Perhaps you could join us one day," Sophia says without taking a breath.

"It's wonderful to meet you Sophia," I say. "I have to leave Tuesday, but I'll get with you when I get back." I feel Matt squeeze my elbow and I wonder what that was for.

"Tell me, Ivy, if you could make one of your books into a movie with Spirit here as the male lead, which book would it be?" Sophia asks.

I think for a few seconds and name my seventh book. I look at Matt and say, "I think Spirit would be perfect for the bad guy turned good guy." I look into his emerald eyes and smile shyly because I remember the book very well and Matt would be perfect. The perfect looks, the perfect body, and I would bet my entire fortune that he would be the perfect lover.

"I remember the book, but I'll reread it. If you'll excuse me, we better go talk to some of our other guests." Sophia grabs Enzo's hand and leads him away as he rolls his eyes. I have to laugh.

A voice comes over a loudspeaker and says something in Italian. I look at Matt. "He said dinner is served in five minutes. We better find our table." Matt signals to an usher, who leads us to a table in front of the stage. Matt helps me get seated before sitting down himself, placing his arm across the back of my chair. "I know you won't understand what's said, so I'll signal you when it's time to laugh."

When I look up, I see him smiling at me. "I'm happy my date is Matt Carson tonight," I whisper.

"Me, too," he replies as others join us.

The night's festivities are fun. Matt's way of signaling me is his arm on the back of my chair, touching my back or his hand on my knee. His warmth floods my body, making me weak with desire. I find it hard to concentrate, but when the name Espíritu Libre is announced, Matt stands to roaring applause. My heart swells with pride and tears spring to my eyes as I look up at him. As he sits down, Matt places a soft kiss on my cheek.

Finally, the music begins, and he leads me onto the dance floor. With one hand on my back and the other holding mine, Matt leads me around the dance floor like a dream. When his favorite song comes on, he moves my arms around his neck before placing his hands on my hips. The world slows down and we are the only two people on earth as his nose touches mine and we gaze into each other's eyes. Then a song from 1986 about a lady in red begins.

"I've never heard this song, but it's perfect," Matt whispers. He pulls me so close our bodies are almost one.

The music overtakes me as I run my fingers through Matt's long, dark hair as he caresses me with his eyes. His hands slide up to my bare back. My breath becomes short and I'm hot all over. I wonder how he feels, if the music and/or me are having the same effect on him.

"Let's go home," Matt whispers in my ear, making me shiver with longing. We make our way to the door, stopping to say goodbye to several people. Then we are finally in the car where I take my heels off.

"Put your feet in my lap," Matt says. I do and he massages my tired feet.

"That feels so good," I sigh.

"When we moved to Spain, my dad always sent enough money for my mom and me to live on. Mom wanted me to go to the best schools, so she worked three jobs. When she came home late at night, I would rub her tired feet," Matt says.

"Your mother loves you very much," I reply.

"Yes. I can't wait for you to meet her. She'll love you." That's all the conversation we have until we reach the apartment.

"Would you like a glass of wine?" Matt asks when we walk in.

"Yes, please." I drop my shoes, wrap, and clutch on the kitchen island and climb ungracefully onto a stool. Matt pours us a glass of wine and sits mine in front of me as I begin pulling hairpins out. "I don't think I'll ever get all these pins out," I say with a laugh, trying to ease the tension I feel in the room.

Matt hands me his phone. "Would you program that song into my playlist? I'll be right back." He hurries out of the room. In a few minutes, he returns and stands behind me.

"Let me help you," he says. "I've had this problem before with my hair." He massages my head as he searches for the pins. When he's satisfied he's found them all, he brushes my hair. "Why didn't you tell me you're leaving Tuesday?" he asks quietly.

Ah, so that's the reason for the tension. "Matt, I didn't know until this afternoon. I didn't see you before we left and then I got so caught up in the evening's excitement I forgot. I apologize."

"Is it necessary for you to leave so soon?"

"Yes, my publisher has booked talk show appearances, book signings, and other things. You know how it is. I'll get home just in time to do laundry, pack, and fly to Los Angeles."

"How long will it take?" he asks.

"I'm not sure, really. I'd have to say four to six weeks. The book awards are in New York City one month from today. If I'm booked for other events, it may be longer."

"Okay. There I'm finished. I'll see you in the morning," he says, handing me the brush and pins. He drinks his wine in one gulp and I see a frown on his beautiful face.

"Would you unzip me first?" I ask, sliding off the stool. Matt steps behind me and slowly unzips the dress, his hands grazing my back softly as he does. When he's finished, he turns around and leave me alone in the room. I gather my things with one hand and hold my dress up with the other, making my way to my bedroom.

Mateo's door opens as I pass by. "You've fallen in love with him, haven't you?"

I look down at the floor. "Yes," I whisper. "Am I that obvious?"

"Only to me, but perhaps you should be to Matt," Mateo says, closing his door.

Once in my room, I undress quickly and climb into bed, falling into a restless sleep.

Chapter 20

I hardly slept so I'm up early. I hate the idea of Vi leaving, so I pick up the newspaper Mateo brought up and glance at the front page. There taking up half the page is a picture of Vi and me last night at the fundraiser. The picture is in color and she looks radiant. I read the story, and it doesn't help my mood.

"What are you frowning about?" Vi's soft voice asks as she walks up next to me. I hand her the paper. She studies the picture and then looks at me. "You are so handsome it makes me breathless," she says. "Would you read the story to me?" That's Vi. Always one to think of others. Unselfish and so undeserving of someone like me. I clear my throat and read the article aloud.

The article states I told the press her name was Ivy. The reporter that wrote the story claims he was up late researching the beautiful woman in the red dress. He identified her as Ivy Webber, one of the most sought after bestseller authors of romance novels in the US. The story is continued on the next page that I hadn't looked at. On the second page are pictures of Vi. There's Vi at one of my book signings. Then there is one of us walking down the street last week with my arm around her shoulder as we pretended to be tourists, and one of us dancing in the rain. The article suggests Vi is the newest of a long string of beautiful women in my life. The article ends with a statement that Vi is older than me.

I look at Vi, and she's smiling. "Well, I guess the cat's out of the bag. Handsome actor and his old lady."

"I'm sorry, Vi."

"For what? We knew this would happen one day. At least now everyone knows who I am. I'm not ashamed or embarrassed. Are you?" Vi's eyes search mine for an honest answer.

"I'm not sorry at all. I'm glad people know. Now you won't have to duck in the car to hide your face, and we won't have to sneak out the back door when we leave. I'm proud to be seen with you. I always have been."

"Then why are you so antsy this morning?" Vi asks.

"Because your privacy here has gone up in smoke. Now photographers will probably follow you around when you leave the building."

"Matt." I place my hand on his shoulder. "I'm used to it. It happens a lot when I travel at home. Please, don't worry about me. Now, why don't you take the boat out and relax today?"

"Will you come with me? It will be our last day together. I have to go to Viterbo tomorrow for the entire day."

Vi smiles at me. "I would like that very much. Would you be able to take me to the airport Tuesday morning?"

"Of course, I will. I wouldn't miss it. Let's scrounge up some food and water to take with us," I say, as my mood lifts a little.

After we gather up some food, bottles of water, and a nice bottle of wine, we change clothes. I text Mateo, telling him to cancel or reschedule anything I have Tuesday morning so we can take Vi to the airport.

"Shall we go out the front door or the back door?" I ask Vi when she returns to the living area wearing a low cut tank top and very thigh revealing shorts, making my body react instantly.

"Let's go out front," Vi says with a laugh.

When I open the front door, I see several reporters waiting for us. I wave and two yell out questions I answer in Italian. Suddenly, an American voice yells, "hey Ivy". I see her search for the owner of the voice and when her eyes find him; she smiles.

"Good morning," Vi tells him.

"Ivy, congratulations on your latest book reaching #1. How do you feel about that?"

"It feels wonderful that the readers enjoy my work. I appreciate everyone that takes time out of their busy lives to read my books."

"What is your relationship with Espíritu Libre?" he asks.

Vi looks up at me and then at the reporter. "We are friends. Espíritu and I share a common interest in his foundation's work for Alzheimer's and dementia patients here in Europe. Maybe you should write about that instead of me," Vi suggests. "The ideas behind the foundation are intriguing and the US could learn a great deal from his work." She gives the reporters a wave as Mateo leads us to the car. Once inside, we are off to the dock.

"Thank you for mentioning the foundation," I say once we pull away from the curb.

Vi takes my hand and looks directly at me with a huge smile. "Your work is far more important than I will ever be, Matt. While I'm gone, perhaps you can think of a way I can help."

"You just did, sweetheart."

CHAPTER 21

E ven though I've only been on the boat once, Matt trusts me to remember everything he taught me. Thank goodness, I do because it doesn't take any time at all before we are headed out to sea. I can tell something is still bothering Matt because he stands on deck at the front of the boat. While I steer from the back. He hasn't spoken to me since we left the car.

Matt's back is to me, and I watch as he pulls his shirt over his head. I nearly combust as I stare longingly at the sculpted muscles of his back and shoulders. Matt motions for me to increase our speed. When I do, he removes the hairband from his hair and his long, wavy locks fly in the wind behind him. I lick my lips. We cross the waves of a passing boat and Matt's thigh and calf muscles stretch as he works to maintain his balance. Okay, so now I'm beyond hot and wet. I'm so busy staring at this perfect man, I get off course.

"Vi, get back on course," Matt yells above the sound of the wind without turning around. I look down and turn the wheel, hoping he doesn't have any idea what distracted me. "Slow down. I'm going to put the sails up." I do as I'm told and try to pay attention to the course, but my mind wanders to running my hands over Matt's naked body.

"Vi, the course," Matt yells, but this time he turns and looks at me while I' still licking my lips.

"Don't worry about me. I can handle it," I yell back, trying to convince myself more than him.

Once all the sails are hoisted, I turn the engines off and the boat glides through the water. Matt continues to stay up front. This goes on for about two hours. I look around and don't see land on either side of us. Matt has remained up front and has been sitting down for quite some time.

"I need to pee," I yell. I've held it as long as I can. Matt stands and makes his way to me and the wheel. "I'm sorry. I just can't wait any longer," I say when he reaches me. Matt doesn't say a word. He just takes the wheel from me and I go downstairs to the bathroom. When I return, I hand him a bottle of water and turn to sit in the chair on the opposite side of the boat. Matt grabs my arm and pulls me to him.

"You belong beside me," he growls in a low voice, looking into my eyes. Matt places me between himself and the wheel. Next, he jumps into the captain's chair and lifts me onto his lap. "This is the way it should be," he whispers into my ear as he places one hand on the wheel and the other at my waist. I lean my head back on his shoulder and take deep breaths, inhaling his scent and that of the sea.

After several minutes, Matt says, "take the wheel, Vi. I'm going to lower the sails and drop the anchor." We work together as a team with no words spoken. Once the boat is still, Matt goes into the galley. A few minutes later, he returns with our bag of food and the bottle of wine. He heads to back to the front of the sailboat and sits down.

"Vi, come here and bring our phones with you." I grab the phones and walk to him. Matt is leaning his back against the largest mast and his legs are spread apart. He holds my hand to steady me and pulls me into the space between his legs.

I open the bag of food while Matt opens the bottle of wine. "Oh, I forgot the glasses," he says with a small laugh.

"I think we can share the bottle," I reply and instantly my mind says yeah, let's do that. Then my lips can be where yours were. I shake my head to clear my thoughts. Next, I set all the food in my lap until the bag is empty. Then I spread the food out next to Matt's leg and lay the food on it. Matt offers the bottle of wine to me and I take a sip before handing it back to him.

"You hold on to it for now," he says. Then, Matt feeds us one bite at a time. When he feeds me a chocolate-covered strawberry, I notice the heat from his hand has melted the chocolate. I pull his fingers down to my mouth and lightly begin sucking the chocolate away. A feral moan escapes Matt's mouth as I suck each fingertip, unable to see him.

"Vi," he whispers into my ear. Instantly, the area below my waist activates and I'm powerless to stop the advancing wetness. I want to turn around, push this man to the deck, and climb on top of him. I want to ravish him until I can no long move. Instead, I release his hand and take a long cooling sip of wine. Sip? Lol! I took a large gulp and then offered the bottle to Matt. He clears his throat and takes a large gulp himself before handing me the bottle.

"Do you have your schedule on your phone?" Matt asks. I nod. "Would you mind sharing it with me and I'll share mine with you? I'm not trying to stalk you. I would like to know where you are and what you're doing."

"Okay, but let's put it in for the time zones we will be in." As Matt tells me his, I enter it into my phone. I notice it is only one month's calendar. "Don't you have anything else?" I ask.

"Not yet. I got word this morning that we begin filming in three months in a small town in Sicily. I typically schedule little because I have a lot of things to do to get ready before then."

"Oh, I understand. Just a minute," I say as my phone pings. "It's Grace, my assistant." Grace is texting me, wanting to know my arrival time back at the apartment so she can meet me there. I give her my best guess. "Now, shall we continue?"

Matt programs all my events, dates, and times into his calendar. Then between the two of us using apps on our phones, we convert the times to the Rome time zone.

"Wow, Vi. You are traveling the entire US in four weeks," Matt says.

"I know. I won't go home at all. Grace will be with me part of the time to help with laundry, bring me fresh clothing, etc. I'd be lost without Grace. She helps me keep my sanity."

"Like Mateo does me?"

"Exactly," I reply.

"Tell me about this award thing in New York City," Matt says.

"It's like the Oscars for book authors only on a much smaller scale. They give awards to the best authors in their genre, cover designers, illustrators, and so on. The last is award is for a book of the year."

"Have they have nominated you for an award?"

I blush because I feel like I'm bragging about myself, which I hate. "Well, yes. Best author in the romance category, best cover designer, and book of the year. Competition is fierce."

"That's fantastic. I guess that's why you chose the red dress, huh?"

"No. Sometimes, I like to dress up just to remind myself that I am a woman," I answer honestly.

"You are the only one that needs to be reminded of that," Matt whispers in my ear. Yeah, open flood gates once again as his breath tickles my ear and chills run down my spine. "I saw the way men looked at you last night. You have no concept of just how beautiful you are."

"You are too kind, Matt. I'm just me."

"Lean back against me and let's enjoy the quiet," Matt says. I do, and his arms wrap around me in a protective cocoon. We watch the waves, listen to the various birds flying around, and wave at passersby. Two boats come near and we see people taking pictures of us. "I guess we'll be on the front page again tomorrow."

"I hope so," I say with a yawn.

CHAPTER 22

I hold on to Vi tightly, hoping this way I can keep her and she won't leave me. I know it won't work because she's dedicated to her craft like I am. In some ways, we are similar. We put ourselves out into the public eye and fight to maintain control of our private lives. I want my public and private life to include her, but I don't know how to make her understand that. I have until Tuesday morning to figure it out.

Since I now have her schedule, I'll keep up with her as she travels. I'll watch her TV interviews, podcasts, whatever every chance I get, even if it means going without sleep. I don't expect I'll sleep much anyway without her nearby or next to me.

Leaning my head back, my mind wanders over things I need to do. It is too far to travel between Sicily and Rome twice a day, so I need a house near the town where we will be filming. I'll need a car and a housekeeper. I need Vi, and I need her to come back when her book tour ends, and I need her to promise me she will come back. At some point, I need to make her understand I don't want to be just friends anymore. I want it all.

Vi stirs in my arms. "I must have dozed off," she says in a quiet voice. Her beautiful red mane brushes my face as she turns her head to look at me. The scent of her, vanilla and cinnamon, grabs my heart and pumps blood below my waist. I have to lift her off me before she realizes the growing activity in my shorts.

"You did. That's okay, but it's getting late. We need to head back now." I stand and offer to help her up.

"You go ahead," she says. "I'll clean up. No wonder I dozed off. We drank the entire bottle of wine." No, sweetheart, I think. I drank most of it, trying to keep from losing my mind about you leaving. I nod and head back to start the engines and raise the anchor.

Mateo and I have been on the road all day. I left Antonio with Vi to help her pack or anything else she might need before she leaves tomorrow morning.

"You've been quiet all day and all night," Mateo says as we pull into the parking garage. "You're going to miss her." I nod. "She'll come back or you could go get her at some point. Didn't you say she had an awards thing and was planning to wear that red dress?" I nod again. "It would be a shame for another man to touch her in that dress."

"Are you trying to kill me?" I ask in a quiet voice.

"No, Matt. I'm trying to plant a seed in your mind. One that I can help you with if you'll let me."

"I don't have a clue what you're talking about."

Mateo laughs. "I know you don't. That's why I recorded what I said. I'll send it to you. Maybe, if you listen to it enough, you'll figure it out."

The apartment is dark and quiet as it should be at 11:00 pm. I quickly shower, grab a small box out of my pants pocket, and head to Vi's bedroom. I hear her soft breathing as I sit down on the edge of the bed and I brush a few stray hairs from her face. She opens her eyes.

"Matt, thank goodness you're home safe. I missed you today," Vi says in her sleepy voice.

"Sit up," I say. "I have something for you." As she does, I turn on the bedside lamp and hand her the box. She opens it and tears fill her eyes.

"Matt, it's beautiful." The box contains a sailboat charm on a long chain. If I estimated correctly, the charm should lie between Vi's breasts. "Will you put it on for me?" she asks, turning her upper body to give me access to the back of her neck. I push the hair away. Then I drape the necklace around her neck, fasten it, and place a soft kiss on her bare shoulder.

"I hope the charm will help you remember our times on the boat," I say. Vi nods.

"I have something for you too." Vi reaches under her pillow and pulls out a small box, handing it to me. I open the box. It contains a tiny silver box with what looks like a drop of water inside. "It's a real rain drop. I know you don't care for jewelry, so I thought maybe you could carry it in your pocket and remember when we danced in the rain."

"Thank you, Vi. I will carry it with me always and never forget that afternoon." I pause and then touch her silky cheek. "Can I hold you tonight?" Vi doesn't say a word. She slides to the other side of the bed and lifts the covers. I crawl in and take her into my arms. "Promise me you'll come back," I whisper.

"I do, Matt. I'll be back."

I get up early the next morning and creep into my bedroom. I slept well, and I think Vi did, too. She felt so wonderful in my arms, like her body was made to be there. We've slept together several nights now and never even kissed, but that didn't stop me from wanting to kiss her and make love to her. It didn't take me long to realize I didn't want sex with her. I wanted hot, passionate, mind-altering love making.

I haven't even thought about other women since my mistake with Marisol. Looking back now, I realize just how big a mistake that was because she got the part for the female lead in my new show. I've ignored her calls and texts. Hopefully, she finally got the hint because I haven't heard from her in a few days.

After showering and dressing, I walk into the kitchen and see Vi's suitcases sitting by the elevator. She hands me a cup of coffee with a sad smile.

"This is harder than I thought it would be," she murmurs. I nod and turn around, trying to hide the wetness in my eyes. Mateo and Antonio walk into the kitchen quietly.

"It's time to go," Mateo says.

Vi walks over to Maya and gives her a big hug, which surprises me. Maya and I never discuss personal things, but I guess she has developed a soft spot for Vi because tears flow down her cheeks. The two women speak a few words in Italian. Then Vi walks over to Antonio and gives him a big hug. She says something to him in Spanish and he kisses her forehead.

"Okay, Mateo, I guess I'm as ready," Vi says. He nods, picks up her suitcases, and disappears into the elevator. I pick up Vi's tote bag while she grabs her purse. I take her hand and we enter the elevator together. We hold hands on the way to the airport, but don't talk. Mateo keeps glancing at me in the rearview mirror as if trying to use ESP and tell me something.

At the airport, Mateo gets Vi's suitcases and prepares to carry them inside. I tell him no. I'll take them. Vi hugs Mateo tightly and a few tears escape down her cheeks. She wipes them away as she backs away from him.

With a suitcase in each hand, I follow Vi into the airport and check in her bags. I grip her hand and we walk toward security. Suddenly, several women appear out of nowhere, calling my name. I stop and address the women in Italian and then continue walking with Vi.

"What did you tell them?" she asks.

"I told them I wanted to tell my friend goodbye and then I would return to take pictures with them," I answer.

"That was very nice of you."

"I know, because I'm a nice guy." I give Vi my biggest smile. She rolls her eyes at me. I look around and spot a family-friendly restroom. I pull Vi toward it, open the door, and push her inside. Immediately, I say. "I want you to come back as soon as possible."

"I know, and I promised I would."

"That's not good enough." Confusion fills Vi's face. "Do you remember what I said in the alleyway about kissing an older woman?"

"Yes, that makes sense now, since you start filming soon," Vi answers.

"I was talking about you, sweetheart." Vi's mouth opens in an "O" and I take my chance. My mouth is quickly on her perfect lips. My tongue into her sweet mouth. She tastes like she smells, like sugar cookies. Pouring all my feelings and passion into the kiss, I feel Vi's lips respond. My mind whirls and my body heats like never before. Her hands grab my hair and pull my lips closer to hers, and we are fused together. One kiss leads to another and another and another. Each time, the kiss becomes more, so much more. I pull Vi closer so she can feel my hardness, my desire for her.

After several minutes, I take a step back but keep my nose is touching hers. Vi's hands are still tangled in my hair. We are both out of breath. We stare into each other's eyes. "I want more," I whisper through my panting. "Much, much more."

"I do, too," Vi says and pulls my lips back to hers. Several minutes later, Vi releases my hair. "I have go," she says against my lips.

"I know. Did I convince you to come back?" I ask. I have to know for my sanity. Vi nods, backs up, grabs her bags she dropped on the floor, and places her hand on the doorknob.

"I'll return as soon as I satisfy all my commitments." She opens the door and steps out while I pull my shirttails out of my pants to hide the bulge I have. Then I walk to the waiting women for selfies and autographs. I look up to find Vi watching me at the entrance to security. I smile and she places her hand on her heart.

CHAPTER 23

As I settle into my small cubicle known as first-class seating, my phone notifies me I have a message from Matt.

"Did it tickle?" I laugh aloud, causing my neighbors to look at me as if they are flying with a nutcase.

"I don't know. My mind was elsewhere." I reply.

"Where?"

"I really don't think I need to answer that question?"

"The same place mine was?"

"Probably."

"Please let me know when you get home, sweetheart."

"Will do." I have to stop then because I have to put my phone on airplane mode.

I sit in the waiting room of the first TV show I'm appearing on in a few minutes. I feel like I haven't stopped since I got back from Rome. Thank goodness for Grace. She met me at the apartment and took care of so many things while I slept. My publisher has crammed more commitments into my month. She wanted to book me into more events, taking me into the following month, but I refused. After the awards show, I'm going home for a few days to rest and then make plans to return to Rome.

Matt and I have texted several times during the days and nights and we talk every day. I know he's as busy as I am, so I'm thankful for the time we do share. Finally, I'm called to the stage and I take a calming breath.

The questions the host asks are a repeat of shows of the past. We talk about my book, my motivation, and my history. But then, the interview takes a different turn. One that I already prepared myself for.

"Ivy, I understand you just got back from a vacation in Rome and you metEspíritu Libre while you were there," the TV host says.

"Yes, I did. He's a delightful man and very popular in Europe," I reply. The host then shows a picture of Matt and explains who he is to the American audience.

The host turns to me. "I recently saw pictures of the two of you together frequently." I almost roll my eyes to myself.

"Yes, I was very interested in a foundation Espíritu created regarding care for Alzheimer's and dementia patients. He and I both have had family members with the disease." I don't give the host a chance to ask another question. I jump right into the work Matt's foundation is doing and state that other countries, including the US, could learn from the foundation's work. Then, I announce to the world via national television that "all the proceeds from the sale of my new book will go to the foundation." The audience goes wild, and the host says our time has ended and thanks me for coming.

I walk out of the TV station and into the limo, waiting to take me downtown to a book signing event. Bless Grace's heart.

There are snacks in the car and my favorite diet soda. With my drink in one hand and a granola bar in the other, I lean my head back against the seat. Well done, Vi, I say to myself. My phone pings, breaking up the silence in the car. I'm thrilled to see it is Matt.

"You didn't have to do that."

"Were you watching? You are supposed to be sleeping."

"Of course I was watching. I wanted to see my sweetheart. But you didn't have to do what you did."

"I did it because I wanted to and I believe in you and what you do." Several seconds of silence pass. "Did you fall asleep on me?" Several more seconds pass. I decide Matt fell asleep and toss my phone on the seat next to me. Ping.

"No, I'm still here. My manager called me to tell me all our social media pages are going crazy with people asking for information on the foundation and how to donate."

"Matt, that's wonderful."

"No, you're wonderful," he replies.

"Get ready, because I'm talking about the foundation every chance I get."

"I need to go, sweetheart. Miss you!!!!!!"

I text Grace. "Call my lawyer and publisher. I think I started something big."

The month flies by with me waking up in a different city every day. My phone calls with Matt have become fewer, but we still text several times a day. Thanks to me, he's busier than ever. The foundation has been inundated with requests from researchers, pharmaceutical companies and potential investors. They want to meet and tour the warehouse. Money is pouring in and Mateo has been searching for another warehouse in Italy. That's the good news. The bad news is that Maya's husband passed away suddenly. It breaks my heart. I ask Matt what I could do and his response was that he's taking care of things.

Finally, I arrived in New York City last night and slept until noon. Grace is here and will attend the awards program, but she can't sit with me. I complain about the two-bedroom suite my publisher booked for me and the fact that it is a waste since Grace is staying on another floor. Grace pacifies me by saying her husband took vacation time to come with her and will be her date tonight. She hurries me off to my appointment to get my nails, hair, and makeup done.

Finally, I'm back at the hotel and Grace is there to help me get dressed. She brought my red dress with her when she flew in several days ago.

"I suppose I'm stuck with some nitwit for a date tonight," I say, ask I slip the dress on. Thankfully, Grace is already dressed.

"I met him while you were gone. He seems like a nice guy," Grace replies.

"You always say that, Grace. You even said that about the idiot last year."

Grace laughs. "Is it my fault he couldn't keep his hands off of you?"

"No, but you could have been single, so he could have bothered you instead. You are closer to his age. OMG! Did Veronica set me up with a fossil this time?"

"No, Vi. He's fine. He's very handsome. I think you'll like him. Okay, I think we're ready. I heard a knock on the door. Let me see if that's your date. I gave my husband valet duty." Grace leaves the room with a laugh.

Looking in the mirror, I'm pleased with what I see looking back at me. I wore my hair down tonight. I reach for my necklace and pull the sailboat charm from between my breasts. It doesn't go with my dress, but I haven't taken it off since Matt put it around my neck. I'm not about to take it off now. Grace sticks her head in to tell me my escort is here and closes the door. I take a deep breath, grab my wrap and clutch, and prepare to face the music.

"I'm coming," I yell through the door. As I turn the doorknob, music plays the song about the woman in the red dress. I jerk the door open and there stands Matt, dressed in his tux. The sight of him takes my breath away. I vaguely hear Grace say something about seeing me in the car.

"Matt!"

"Hello, sweetheart. I want you to know I'm not a nitwit, idiot or fossil," he says with a huge grin. He walks over to me and presses his perfect lips to mine. I pour every desire I have ever wanted to feel for a man into the kiss, and Matt returns tenfold.

"We better think about going or we may never leave this suite," he says as he takes a step back. He reaches into his pocket, pulls out the velvet-covered box, and opens it. "You forgot this," he says, as his eyes twinkle. I turn and hold my hair up so he can place the necklace around my neck. He kisses my shoulder and I shiver.

"I've been meaning to ask you. Are those shivers you get when I touch you good shivers?" he whispers in my ear.

"One day, I'll show you what those shivers do to me," I reply.

"I can't wait. You have your necklace on."

"I haven't taken it off," I say. I reach for the earrings and as I put them on, Matt pulls out the little box with the rain drop I gave him.

"I have it with me all the time and I even sleep with it," he says as I look at his palm. "Let's go, woman. No one touches you but me tonight. Understand?" I nod. Matt picks my stuff up off the floor and hands it to me. Then he offers his hand and we go to the limo. The limo driver opens the door and there sits Mateo, with Grace and her husband. Mateo leans over and kisses my cheek, smiling from ear to ear.

CHAPTER 24

I swear Vi looks more beautiful tonight than she did the first time I saw her in that red dress. My heart stopped beating the minute I saw her, but she quickly jump started it when I kissed her. As far as I'm concerned, this woman will be mine for eternity. I pray I don't screw it up.

The venue is smaller than I expected when we pull up to the valet parking, but it looks great. I help Vi out of the car, and they greet us with flashes of light. I look over my shoulder to see Mateo, Grace, and her husband behind us as we enter the building. Grace and her husband leave us, but Mateo stays a short distance away.

Inside there is an area for photographs and interviews. Vi and I are led there by two distinguished people, also dressed in tuxedos. I hold Vi close as we pose for pictures. Afterward we go to the interview area.

"Ivy, has does it feel to be nominated again? Ivy, what do you think your chances are? Ivy, when's your next book coming out? Ivy, who designed your dress?" Vi smiles and answers each question politely.

Then, **"Espíritu!"** someone yells. I hold up my hand.

"Folks, I'm not here to answer questions tonight. I'm here to support this beautiful woman and celebrate her accomplishments as an astute novelist and a kind and generous person," I say. Then I lean over and kiss Vi's cheek.

After a few more questions for Vi, they usher us to our table, stopping along the way for greetings and introductions. I can easily tell that Vi is well liked and respected by her peers. We are seated with Vi's publisher, Veronica, her brother and partner in the business, their spouses, and Vi's lawyer and publicist. After the introductions, Vi and I sit down. I place my hand on her bare thigh.

"Are you nervous, sweetheart?" I lean over and ask.

"A little. At least I don't have to signal you when to laugh," she says with a smile that makes my world brighter than any sunshine ever could.

During dinner, the conversation is lively and upbeat. I learn that Veronica's brother actually discovered Vi and signed her to her first contract. Finally, it's time for the award presentations. It starts off slow for me because it goes by genre. I glance at the program and notice the romance genre is the last. Oh well, I think. That gives me more time to touch the beautiful woman at my side. I alternate resting my hand on her thigh, brushing her hair off her shoulder, and placing my arm on the back of her chair. Whenever I change my position, Vi looks at me and takes my breath away.

The announcer states the romance genre is next and I applaud, probably louder than I should, and everyone at the table laughs. The illustrator award is first. A couple two tables over wins. Next is the cover designer. I swell with pride as Vi's name is announced as a nominee. Her latest book cover flashes on the screen, and I'm amazed at the talent Vi has. I knew she wrote books, but I did not know she had artistic talent as well. They announce someone else as the winner and I'm disappointed, but Vi, well, she's Vi. She stands and congratulates the person as they walk past us toward the stage. I know she's sincere.

Next is the Romance Novel of the Year award. Vi's knee shakes beneath my hand and I squeeze it gently. I look over to the side where Mateo stands. He looks at me, smiles, and crosses his fingers. As they announce the nominees, the book covers appear on the screen and they read a description of the book.

"And the winner is Ivy Webber!"

Vi's hand flies to her mouth. I stand and assist her out of her seat. She slowly makes her way to the stage and accepts the award. As I watch my siren steps to the microphone, I feel tears come to my eyes. She begins her speech by thanking all her readers and everyone else involved in the book. Vi even thanks Grace.

But then she looks directly into my eyes and says something that rocks my world. "Spirit, mi corazón te pertenece." That's Spanish, for my heart belongs to you. My chest swells, my breath hitches, and yeah, I see hearts, and flowers, and rainbows—all that lovey dovey stuff. Vi leaves the podium and makes her way back to the table. I stand, intending to kiss her on the cheek, but she turns her head and my lips end up on hers for a second before we sit down. I can't take my eyes off Vi and miss the announcement for the Book of the Year nominees, but she nudges my knee with hers.

"The winner is Ivy Webber!" That's all I hear. I don't hear the name of the book, the publishing company, nothing but Vi's pen name. The audience goes wild and stands clapping, whistling, and when Vi steps on stage, several cat calls, much to my dismay. Veronica and her brother say a few words first. Then Vi takes over the podium. She basically repeats all the people she thanked minutes before. Finally, she talks about Alzheimer's and dementia and her family members that suffered from it. She then asks everyone to remember the caregivers and how hard the journey of the disease is for them.

I watch as the woman I love walks down the steps toward me with tears in her eyes. At that moment, I don't care what anyone thinks. I wrap my arms around Vi and grasp her tightly. I understand her feelings because I've lived it too in my family.

The evening has ended. People surround the table congratulating Vi. She offers words of encouragement to her fellow authors and praise to those that didn't win. We head to the door but are stopped for the last questions and photos. They want Vi holding her trophies, but she wants me in the photos as well. I hand her wrap and clutch to Mateo. I stand so close I could almost be in the dress with her.

Grace and her husband wait for us at the valet station. She hugs Vi tightly and cries with joy. When the limo arrives, the five of us head to the hotel, bypassing the after parties. Grace and her husband go to their room. Mateo hugs and congratulates Vi before heading to his room. Vi and I go to the spacious two-bedroom suite. Mateo had called ahead, so champagne and chocolate-covered strawberries are sitting on a table in the middle of the sitting room. I lift Vi onto a stool and remove her shoes, knowing her feet hurt.

"I'm disappointed," I say.

"Why?"

"They didn't have dancing," I answer with a wink. I lift Vi off the stool, take my phone out of my pocket, and hit my favorite playlist. It only has two songs on it. I press the repeat button. Then I take Vi into my arms as the music begins and we dance. I do not know how long we've danced or how many times the songs were repeated. I know that I'm totally lost in this red-haired woman.

Vi backs away and says, "let's sit down and talk." She sits on the sofa and I open the champagne, pouring us each a glass. I pull an ottoman in front of her and sit down.

"Matt, how did you manage to get away and make all this happen?"

I laugh and say, "I can't take much of the credit. I had the idea, but Grace and Mateo made it happen, so I just did what I was told."

"Why did you come?"

"I came for two reasons, both of them selfish. I didn't want any other man around you in that dress. The other reason is that I came to take you home with me. Well," I pause, "not for a few days, anyway. I know you need to rest, so I'm going to Colorado to visit my dad. Next, I'm coming to Tulsa so you can show me around. Then I'll help you pack and take you home."

After setting her glass down, Vi leans forward and takes my face in her hands. "You really want to take me home with you?" she asks quietly.

"I want you with me more than anything in this world. I want you there as my friend, my lover, my everything," I reply. "Things will be different, though. When we film, I'll be working twelve, eighteen, or maybe twenty hours per day. We'll live in a different place as well, but I'm sure you will love it. I was hoping you might help with the foundation in my absence."

"Okay, but I sense a hitch in your plan," Vi says hesitantly.

"There is a hitch. As much as I want you, I need you to be absolutely sure about it. I'm talking about intimacy." I pause. "When it happens, and I really hope it will, I want it to be special, for you, for me, for us."

"I understand. I'll consider my options and get back to you." Vi grins and winks at me, causing me to laugh. "Now, let's get into those strawberries."

I retrieve the strawberries, and we sit side by side on the sofa talking and feeding each other. Vi's still in her dress, and I'm still in my tuxedo shirt and pants. Like Vi, I shucked the shoes a while ago.

"Vi, when are you leaving here?"

"Grace's husband leaves tomorrow. Then she and I leave Monday morning. We have things to pack."

"If it's okay with you, I'd like to leave Monday as well to see my dad. Then I plan to be with you on Thursday," I say.

"That sounds great. Just let me know your flight schedule and I'll pick you up at the airport."

"There's no need for that. I chartered a plane."

"Why?" Vi asks, confused.

"I didn't know how much you would want to take home and I didn't want to ship anything," I say sheepishly. "Now, I've had an extremely long and exciting day. Can I sleep with you tonight?"

"Do you really have to ask?"

"I didn't want to impose." Vi stands, and I take her in my arms. "Sweetheart, I'm so proud of you. I am glad I could be here tonight to see you get the recognition you deserve." I kiss her like a starved man. Well, I am starved. I haven't been near her in a month.

CHAPTER 25

Matt is so sweet. He helps Grace and I pack up everything from clothes to awards to books, etc. He goes with Grace to the shipping store down the street to ship home everything we don't want to take on the plane.

Monday morning, I say goodbye to Matt before checking out of the hotel. Well, truthfully, it was more of a making out session. Anyway, he leaves afterward to go to a smaller airport where his chartered plane waits. Grace and I go to JFK for our direct flight to Tulsa instead of Oklahoma City because it was easier for Grace and her husband.

Grace and I talk nonstop on the flight, mostly about Matt, but also about the book I was should be writing. I explain I have no idea what to write, but Grace assures me it will come to me.

When I arrive home at 1:30 pm, I send Grace home. I unpack, do laundry, and gather clothes to take to the dry cleaners. Hungry, I go to the kitchen where my competent assistant had stocked the fridge and pantries with fresh food. I make a sandwich and sit on the sofa to take a cleansing breath, eat and text Matt that I made it home safely.

"So Matt wants me to go home with him," I say aloud. "Is that what I really want?" My mind relives every moment spent with Matt. I admit it was some of the best times of my life.

Now, I know he has powerful feelings toward me and it's not about sex after our talk Saturday night. But can I make a life with him? Can I commit, or can he? Well, I have a couple of days to think about it before he gets here.

Matt flies directly into Tulsa, so I pick him up at the airport at 4:30 pm. He tells me he had a delightful visit with his dad over dinner at my favorite Mexican restaurant. Then we go home and snuggle before heading off to bed. Matt holds me in his arms and we both sleep peacefully.

I get up first Friday morning and make a full breakfast for us. Matt wonders into the kitchen, takes me in his arms, and kisses me with a vengeance.

"Have you decided, sweetheart?" he murmurs in my ear.

"I have, but I have several things to do first. When do you want to leave?"

"I'd like to help you with whatever you need and see Tulsa. I think next Friday would be good. How do you feel about that?"

I smile and say, "that sounds perfect."

After breakfast, Matt makes several phone calls while I clean the kitchen and make out a grocery list.

"What are you doing?" he asks, walking up behind me and wrapping me in his arms.

"I'm making out a list. If I'm going back with you, there are food staples this American girl needs to survive."

Matt laughs. "Okay, sweetheart, let's go shopping."

We head to the food store where I buy things like tortilla chips, salsa, enchilada sauce, canned chili, processed cheese (yeah, you see where this is going, don't you?), and different seasonings. Then, we stop and buy boxes and bubble wrap. We stop for lunch and finally go back to the apartment to box all my precious food.

"You didn't have to buy so much, did you?" Matt asks. "You can always have Grace ship more over."

"A woman needs what she needs. By the way, how's Maya?" I ask as I tape a box closed.

"Well, I'm happy to say she's agreed to move to our new home. Her kids are grown and have families of their own. She is lost without her husband, so she agreed a change of scenery might be good for her."

"Matt, you haven't told me about the new apartment or where it is yet. Is it top secret or something?"

Laughing heartily, he says, "it's not top secret, but a surprise. I think you'll be pleased. I am keeping the apartment in Rome for foundation purposes."

"Okay, I can't wait. Will it be ready when we get back to Rome?"

"Mateo and Antonio are overseeing the move as we speak. That's why I'm not in a rush. I want everything perfect when you walk in."

I can't help but smile at him. "Okay, let's order in for dinner. What do you want?"

During dinner and afterwards, Matt wants to know about my one month trek across the US. When I finish, he tells me about his book tours and nightclub visits. We both have been very busy. Matt also tells me his foundation purchased another warehouse outside of Rome and construction has started on it. The first facility was completed and is at 100% occupancy, which is exciting news. He again thanks me for donating my book proceeds to the foundation.

Finally, we talk about the weather where we will live so I can decide if I need to buy clothes. Matt explains the temperatures and the seasons, which sounds perfect and no, I don't need more clothes. But I need something sexy or many things sexy. While Matt goes to the bathroom, I text Grace.

"I need to go shopping in OKC at a lingerie store."

"When?" she asks.

"I would like to go tomorrow, but need to do something with Matt."

"I'll talk to my husband."

Several seconds later, Grace texts, "All taken care of. Frank will pick Matt up tomorrow at 11:00 am and drop me off. He'll take Matt to a sports bar that shows soccer games on their big screens."

"Perfect. Thanks!"

When Matt returns, I say, "guess what! Frank wants to take you to a sports bar tomorrow so the two of you can watch soccer games."

"That sounds like fun. I like Frank very much. What time is he picking me up?"

"At 11:00. He's dropping Grace off and we'll go shopping while you're gone." I stand and walk over to a table by the door. "Here's a spare key in case you get back before I do," I say, handing Matt the key.

"Thanks. Now I'm ready to go to bed and snuggle with my woman," Matt says with a devilish grin.

CHAPTER 26

After the pilot and I load Vi's four suitcases and all ten boxes of food and personal items Vi packed, we are finally ready to leave. Thank goodness! I've already been in touch with Mateo this morning, and everything is ready.

The filming of the TV show will take place in Partinico, Sicily. I was able to rent a fully furnished villa on a hill overlooking the Tyrrhenian Sea between Sicily and Italy. The villa is outside of town and will be a fifteen minute drive to work. There is an infinity pool and a guest house. The villa has an office, library, and five bedrooms, one for me, one for Vi, one for Maya, and two for guests. Mateo and Antonio will live in the guest house. Mateo and Maya shopped for linens, dishes, and everything else needed for the house.

Vi and I will fly into Palermo, which is about a forty-five minute drive to the villa. Mateo and Antonio will meet us there with a large SUV that will hopefully carry everything Vi packed. LOL.

The flight will take approximately eighteen hours. We will need to stop in Miami to take on more fuel. Fortunately, I rented a large plane with a bedroom. Vi and I spend our time in there so the additional flight crew can rest in the main cabin. Vi is surprised at the champagne and chocolate-covered strawberries in the room. I surprise her more with the five course dinner and full breakfast I arranged for us. For once, she and I both sleep on the flight and wake refreshed.

Mateo and Antonio greet Vi with enormous hugs, and me with handshakes. Vi looks around excitedly and asks where we are. I tell her Palermo, Sicily. She gives me a gorgeous smile and waits beside the SUV while the three of us men load everything.

"Matt, did she leave anything at home?" Mateo asks, laughing.

"Oh, yeah. This is only a fraction of her belongings. Vi kept her apartment. She said she would worry about it later," I answer.

"Smart woman," Mateo says, but without the smile. That bothers me.

Once we're loaded, we drive to the villa. Mateo stops to key in the gate code as Vi looks around. I smile because we cannot see the villa from the gate. Once at the front of the villa, Vi barely waits for Mateo to stop the SUV before jumping out.

"Oh Matt! This is beautiful. What a wonderful place."

"I'm glad you like it, but there's a lot more to see," I say, placing my hands on her hips. "Let's go. I'll give you a tour." We tour the back first so I can show Vi the view and the pool. I point to a dock in the distance that is visible from the patio.

"Matt, is that your boat?" I nod. Then I take her hand and show her around the house. I haven't seen it since I signed the lease and am pleased with the paintings and décor Mateo and Maya picked out. Maya rushes out of her bedroom and hugs Vi tightly. Tears run down both women's cheeks. Funny thing about some women, I've noticed. Tears and hugs say everything, so words aren't needed.

Finally, I show Vi to her bedroom. "I have a bedroom?" she asks confused, a little frown on her face.

"Only until you are ready to join me in our bedroom, sweetheart. I will not pressure you, but I will sleep with you in yours until that time comes." I take her in my arms and kiss her passionately.

"It will be soon," Vi whispers when we break apart to catch our breath. Then we walk into the kitchen where Maya has lunch prepared for all of us. Vi and I carry our food to the patio while everyone else eats inside.

"When do you start filming?" she asks.

"In thirty days. You and I have two weeks before I have to prepare. We will shoot in the town so it's a fifteen minute drive one way. I want time for us, Vi. I negotiated Sundays off and one week off every two months. Once we shoot, I would like you to go with me sometimes and see what takes place."

"Matt, I would love that," Vi says, covering her hand with mine. "You'll need to show me what you want me to do with the foundation, too."

"I know you need to work on your book, so I'll try not to take too much of your time. The foundation has no board of directors. It's just Mateo and me. You'll need to help him out from time to time. You'll be perfect at it."

CHAPTER 27

The first two days after we arrived were spent in and around the pool and walking the gardens surround the villa. The next day, Matt and I toured the town and surrounding area. When I asked him about me driving, he said one man will drive me wherever I wanted to go. Although the area is safe, he didn't want to risk anything happening to me. We spent the fourth day on Matt's boat, sailing around the coastline of Sicily.

Matt's remaining free days were spent doing whatever he wanted to do. We swam and shopped. We snuggled a lot. Matt slept with me every night, but mentioned nothing about moving into his bedroom permanently. One day, we sailed to Rome, spent the night at the apartment, toured both warehouses, spent another night, and sailed back the next day.

I learned a lot during those two weeks. First, Maya was off all day Tuesday and Thursday afternoons. I eagerly made dinner those nights. We ate dinner as a family. Maya protested at first, but Matt talked to her. At dinner, Maya and I practiced our Spanish, and Antonio and I practiced our Italian. We had a lot of laughs. The most important thing I learned was that Sundays were for soccer. So on Saturdays, Maya and I shopped for snack items. Of course, I made queso with the goodies I had brought and I taught Maya how to make guacamole. Everyone sits in the living area and watches the biggest TV screen I had ever seen and cheers on their favorite teams.

I made my decision to move permanently into Matt's bedroom the Sunday afternoon before he had to begin preparing for his work. He had been swimming before bedtime and while he was taking a shower; I changed into the sexiest negligee I brought. When he came out of the shower wearing only a towel, I was standing with my back to him looking out the floor to ceiling windows. I didn't hear him walk over to me, but when he put his hands on my shoulders and whispered, are you sure, I knew I was.

Matt made slow, genuine love to me from head to toe. I had never experienced the sensations he made my body feel. It was better than anything I had ever imagined or wrote in a book. After several hours, we fell asleep only to wake as the sun rose and start all over again and again and again.

CHAPTER 28

I should start learning the script, but all I want to do is worship Vi's body like I did last night and this morning. I was concerned about making love to her because I had never done it before. But once I started and her body responded, everything fell into place. The woman is a sensual creature who needed the right man to bring everything to the surface. The things she did to me were nothing I had ever experienced. Nothing was sex. It was all pure love, and I will never grow tired of Vi's body, her movements, moans, and whispers.

But I need to work, so after lunch, I walk into the library and close the door. Vi said she was going to move some of her clothes and toiletries to my bedroom and bathroom. Oh, I mean our bedroom and bathroom. As I read over the script, I find changes from the original script and I'm not entirely happy about it. But, it is what it is, and it's my job to bring the character to life. I stay in the library until someone softly knocks on the door. Vi peeks her head in and says dinner in thirty minutes. I nod and smile because it's Vi's night to cook, and she always surprises me.

Each day, I work stopping for lunch only. I quit at dinnertime and enjoy time with my little family. Yes, these people are my family and I love each one of them, especially the red-haired one. My last two weeks before filming passes faster than I like. Days are for working out, studying and memorizing my lines and nights are for loving Vi.

Finally, the first day of work arrives. Mateo and I get up at 5:00 am and work out for an hour and a half. Vi insists on getting up and preparing a hearty breakfast for us. At 7:30, Mateo takes me to the set and returns to the villa to work on foundation issues.

First, there is an introductory meeting with everyone involved. From the makeup artists, costume designers, camera people, etc. to the lowest paid position are required to attend. The only person missing is Marisol. It will be another two months before she needs to be here. Thank goodness. The meeting lasts for three hours. The rest of my day includes meeting with the director, discussing the script and meeting town locals that will be extras on the set. I understand the importance of each person and make a point to talk to each one individually for a few minutes. After all, a TV show can't be made without a team.

Mateo picks me up at 7:00 pm, and we head home. We discuss foundation issues and what Vi can do to help. Mateo suggests creating a board comprised of Vi, me, and himself, and letting Vi be the face of the foundation when I'm unavailable. I agree and plan to discuss it with her after dinner.

"Sweetheart," I begin as we sit by the pool after dinner. "Mateo and I believe it is time to create a board of directors for the foundation. We want you to be on the board."

"Matt, are you sure? I know so little about the workings of the foundation," Vi replies.

"But you are so good with people and can talk to anyone about anything. People love you. We would like you to represent the foundation when I can't, which will be while we are filming."

"I don't know," Vi says as her eyebrows almost meet with a crease forming between them. She stands and paces in front of me.

"Vi, sweetheart, you have a gift with words. You can do the interviews and the tours of the facility. Mateo and I would be proud to have you play a major part in something we both love." I grab her hand as she passes by me and pull her into my lap. "I know you care about the work the foundation is doing."

"But I need to work on my book. I haven't even started because I still don't have any ideas," Vi states.

"You'll have plenty of time to work on your book. Mateo can schedule things to make that happen. Please say yes, Vi. It would mean so much to me."

"Okay, Matt. I'll do my best and try not to disappoint you."

Lifting Vi to her feet, I stand, pick her up, and carry her to our bedroom. We undress each other and make love slowly. When we finish, we lie in each other's arms as moonlight fills the bedroom. I get out of bed and walk to my closet. Vi notices my hand is behind my back when I return. She rises on her elbow. I sit down beside her, still holding my hand behind my back.

"Vi, I haven't told you this before, but I feel now is the time. I love you with my heart, my mind, and my soul. I want you beside every step of the way in life. Whatever the future holds, I want us to make the journey together."

"Matt, I love you so much and want to spend the rest of my life with you. There's only one problem. I can't give you children," Vi says as tears fill her eyes.

"Sweetheart, I've known that from the beginning. Children aren't important to me. There are so many people of all ages that need help. We can do it together." I bring my hand around and open a small box. "I'm not sure either of us is ready to talk about marriage. Our relationship is still young, but I do want to commit the rest of my life to you. Will you accept my commitment and will you commit to me?"

Vi's beautiful blue eyes look directly into mine as the tears now stream down her cheeks. "Yes, Matt. I will commit to be yours now and forever." I take the matching rings from the box and slide Vi's on her finger first. Then she slides mine on. We kiss and make love all over again.

CHAPTER 29

The next five months fly by. Matt and I develop a routine where I make breakfast for him every morning after he works out. It's our time to talk because he returns home from filming the TV show at 8:00 pm or later. He texts me how hungry he is once he gets in the car and I make a wholesome meal, depending on his appetite. No matter how tired he is, we always make love every night.

Sometimes I go with him to watch him act. I don't stay, but for a few hours. Of course, I am shocked to see Ms. Big Boobs as the leading lady, but I accept it. I just can't be there for any kissing or love scenes. Matt assures me he is always covered and the kisses are swift and meaningless.

Mateo meets with the foundation's lawyer and creates a board. I am the director of public relations. Once a month, Mateo and I travel to Rome to meet with potential investors, donors, medical companies, and anyone else that is interested. As Matt promised, it doesn't take much of my time, but I have yet to develop a story for my book. The last time I talked to Grace, I mentioned I may request an extension. She told me to wait. There was still time.

I notice minor changes in Matt at the beginning of the sixth month. He has cut his beautiful hair off to his shoulders. His beard is trimmed very short. Matt says it's for the show's character. Next, he dresses differently. It's more like his TV character with more jewelry and less color. Black seems to be his new norm.

Matt sometimes forgets to text me about dinner and arrives home smelling of alcohol. He isn't a big drinker. Then, he tells me not to get up and make breakfast for him. He and Mateo will pick up something on the way. Finally, our lovemaking at night goes from every night to every other night to twice a week, if I'm lucky. Matt blames it on being tired. Plus, now Sundays are spent watching soccer instead of spending it with me on the boat or doing other things.

On the last Sunday of the month, Matt takes a walk after the games end. It is almost dark. I watch him move past the pool and Mateo intercepts him. I probably shouldn't listen to the conversation, but the voices are loud.

"So, Matt, you're starting this crap all over again," Mateo says.

"What crap?"

"You're getting caught up in your TV character just like before."

"I'm not!" Matt yells.

"Yes, you are. You're dressing like him, acting like him, and drinking like him. You're not paying any attention to Vi."

"It's none of your business," Matt says.

"But it is my business. I'm the one that took you for help the last time and I'll do it again if I have to," Mateo says.

"Just stay out of it, Mateo. I can handle my life and Vi," Matt says, walking off. Mateo turns and sees me standing at the window and shakes his head.

When Matt finally comes to bed, I'm waiting. "Matt, tell me what's going on with you," I say.

"It's nothing."

"Didn't we promise from the beginning that we would be open and honest with each other? I want to know the truth," I state firmly.

"If you really want to know, this isn't working out for me," Matt says, refusing to look at me.

"What do you want, Matt?"

"I want to see other women. I want to have sex with more women than just you."

My entire world just shatters, but instead of crying or arguing, I get out of bed and head to the door.

"Aren't you going to say anything?" Matt asks.

"What's there to say? I know you well enough that when you decide to do something, no one or nothing will change your mind," I answer. I leave the room, softly closing the door behind. Thankfully, I was of sound enough mind to pick up my phone on the way out.

I sit on my bed and text Mateo.

"Can Antonio help me tomorrow?"

"Sure, Vi. I'll tell him to do whatever you need," Mateo replies.

Then I get on the internet and charter a plane for the next day to take me home the next afternoon.

I spend my night crying while I pack my suitcases with the clothes I left in my bedroom. The following morning, I wait until I hear Matt and Mateo leave. Then I pack the clothes I had in Matt's bedroom and the few personal items I brought. I don't pack a single thing that I or Matt bought for me after I arrived. I toss it all into garbage bags that Antonio and I will drop off at a homeless shelter on the way to the airport.

While Antonio carries everything to the rented SUV Mateo kept, I walk into Matt's bedroom. I lay the velvet box containing the sapphire necklace and earrings, the sailboat charm and its chain, and the commitment ring on the table next to Matt's bed. Then, I hug Maya and tell her goodbye and give her an envelope for Mateo. I walk out of the villa with my head held high and climb into the SUV, vowing to never return.

CHAPTER 30

Okay, I got it off my chest. I saw the hurt in Vi's eyes and was surprised she acted the way she did. Well, not really. That's Vi's style. I lie down and feel like a weight has been lifted off my shoulders. Now, I'm free to live my life the way I want to.

Mateo drives me to work the following morning, and I enjoy the silence. The argument we had last night was one we had before. Mateo is wrong. This isn't like the last time when I let my character, Enrique Salas, from **Ama el único camino**, take over my life. Yeah, I became him. Womanizing, drinking, dressing like him, and even absorbing his life style. My mom and Mateo put me into a psychiatric facility for six months. That's not happening this time, I tell myself.

When Mateo stops the car, I tell him not to bother picking me up this evening. I'll let him know when he needs to pick me up. The day is long and I retreat to my trailer to decompress when we finish. Someone knocks on the door and I'm surprised to see it's another actor from the show. He holds up two bottles of whiskey and jerks a finger behind him. Two more actors are behind him, plus three minor female characters from the show. I invite them in and we drink until the wee hours of the morning.

The following day, I wake to my alarm and find one woman in my bed. She's not that good looking, but has a good body, I notice as she turns over.

"Hey, you need to get up," I tell her, shaking her shoulder.

She yawns and says, "good morning. I hope you feel better this morning." She points to me below the waist with a smile.

"What's that supposed to mean?"

"Well, your equipment didn't work last night. Want to try again?"

"No, now get up and leave. We start work in a couple of hours," I say. My equipment didn't work. I don't remember that, I think as I try to remember the night. Heck, I don't even know her name. The woman dresses and leaves quickly. I shower and head down to the set for coffee and pastries, praying someone has ibuprofen.

It's another long day, especially when I've had very little sleep and a hangover that won't let up. When we finish, the guy from the night before shows up with more whiskey and different women at my trailer.

The following morning is a repeat of the day before. A different woman in my bed claiming my equipment didn't work. It must be the whiskey. I have problems trouble remembering some of my lines, but the director is patient. Once the day ends, I text Mateo to come get me. I need fresh clothes.

It's Antonio that picks me up instead of Mateo. Antonio has never been much of a talker, so the drive to the villa is deathly quiet. It is 11:00 pm when we drive up to the front door. Antonio drops me off and drives toward the garage. When I open the front door, the house is eerily quiet and dark. I walk to my bedroom, undress, and quickly shower without turning the bedroom light on.

I'm hungry, but too tired to care, so I drop my towel and climb into bed. My arm automatically reaches over to Vi, but she's not there. Of course, she isn't you, idiot. Not after what you told her. I reach for her pillow to inhale her vanilla and cinnamon scent, but that too isn't there. That's when I realize the sheets have been freshly laundered.

I climb out of bed and return to the bathroom to find nothing belonging to Vi, nor the scent of her body wash or perfume. With only the bathroom light on, I find a pair of shorts and pull them on. I go to the closet, but only find my clothes. I make my way to Vi's bedroom and tap softly on the door. When there's no answer, I open the door. The bed is vacant. I look in the closet. It's totally empty and so is the bathroom. Nothing in the room has Vi's unique scent. I walk through every room of the villa except Maya's bedroom. It's as if Vi had never walked through the front door.

I walk back to my bedroom and sit down on the bed. Next, I turn on the lamp beside the bed. That's where I find the velvet-covered box, the sailboat charm and chain, and the commitment ring. The only three things that prove Vi was ever part of my life. I can't stay here, I quickly decide, so I throw come clothes into an overnight bag and head to the garage. I get in the car and drive back to my trailer on the set of the show.

CHAPTER 31

Grace picks me up at the airport. She can tell by the look on my face and my demeanor not to ask questions. She takes me directly to my apartment and helps me carry my things inside. Finally, she hugs me tightly and leaves me alone.

So what does a fifty-year-old woman whose lover told her she isn't enough for him to do? I cried, didn't eat or bathe, and didn't sleep. I screamed in my pillow and broke every mirror in the apartment so I wouldn't have to look at myself. My doctor was kind enough to do a video visit and prescribed my favorite antidepression medication that numbs me and had it delivered to my door. I turned my phone off before I left Palermo and haven't turned it back on. This went on for a week. Grace popped by twice to check on me and left quickly.

On Monday of the second week, with several days of my medication in my system, I had a talk with myself. This wasn't the first time I had been left with a broken heart, but it would be the last. I cleaned myself up, ate some food Grace was kind enough to bring by, and did what any bestselling romance author would do. I wrote a book.

Yes, I wrote about the last eight months of my life. Oh, I changed the characters' names, their professions, and the foundation to one that helps children. I added several steamy sex scenes that may or may not have happened. Then, I sent the manuscript to Veronica one month before the actual due date. Then, I booked a transpacific cruise to Australia and New Zealand that leaves in one week.

I finally had the nerve to turn my phone on. There were phone calls and messages from several people, but none from Matt, and I wasn't surprised. I deleted all the messages, except one from Mateo. According to the date of the message, it was sent two days ago.

"Vi, I hope you will continue to be involved in the foundation. Your work is excellent and I really need your help. I can handle the next couple of months alone, but I need you desperately after that, if you will agree."

My dear Mateo, the handsome, inked giant that had become a good friend these past months. I really enjoyed my work with the foundation and had several ideas for expansion. I messaged him back.

"Mateo, I would like to stay involved with the foundation, but under one condition. I never want to see or talk to Matt again. I'm leaving on a trip next week and will be gone for one month. Let's discuss when I return."

"Thanks and I understand. I will ensure your condition will be fully met. You have my word. Call me when you get back."

I call Grace and ask her to go shopping with me in two days. I want a brand new wardrobe for my trip and my life. Next, I call my hairdresser and get a shorter hairstyle that will be easier to deal with. Fortunately, she gets me in that day. When I leave the salon, I head straight to a tattoo parlor and have a small broken heart put on the top of my left breast.

The day before I fly to Los Angeles for my cruise, I get an email from Veronica saying she loves the book and has just a few edits. She has attached her edited manuscript. She also included a new contract for two books within the next eighteen months. I ignore the contract, print out the manuscript, and toss it into my tote bag along with my laptop. It will give me something to do on the sea days of the cruise.

When the cruise ends, I check into a hotel in Melbourne and begin booking tours of the area. Since I opted for Wi-Fi on the ship, I could view and choose the ones I wanted for Australia and New Zealand that weren't offered by the cruise line. I order room service and send the revised manuscript to Veronica. I add a note that I would consider the contract, but for now, I just wanted time with no pressure or deadlines.

One month after leaving Tulsa, I arrive back home. The apartment seems so empty and I consider moving, but I really like the area. I decide to purchase all new furniture, linens, dishes, everything and call a decorator. We make an appointment for the following week.

I had plenty of time to think about Mateo's message while I was away. I still have mixed feelings about working with the foundation, but I really love the work it is doing and the part I was involved in. Grabbing my phone, I check the time in Rome, finding it is early evening, so I call Mateo.

"Vi! What a pleasant surprise," Mateo says. "How was your trip?"

"It was wonderful and relaxing. How are you, Mateo?"

"I'm good, just busy with foundation work. Congratulations, by the way."

"For what?" I ask.

"Vi, your book went to #1 the first week it went on sale. Didn't you know?"

I laugh. "No, I've been purposely avoiding all calls and messages. That was the goal of getting away."

Mateo laughs. "I can understand that. I hope you took time to think about my proposal."

Breathing deeply, I ask, "can you really ensure my request?"

"I can."

"Okay, then. I would really like to stay involved and I have a few ideas for expansion if you're interested. I can be in Rome next week if that will work for you."

"That's great news. Can we make it the week after? There are issues here that I need to deal with next week that can't be postponed," Mateo says quietly.

"That's fine. I'll call you once I make all the arrangements. I can't wait to see you again."

"Me either, Vi."

CHAPTER 32

I am in trouble. I can't eat or sleep and I no longer look or act like Matthew Carson. I haven't been able to perform in bed since my last time with Vi. This has led to more drinking. I have trouble remembering my lines and I'm cross with everyone on the set. I can feel them whispering about me behind my back. No one socializes with me and women avoid me. The director is very unhappy with me because the production is behind schedule.

My time is very limited at the villa. I may go home every three or four days and then it's only to sleep and get fresh clothes. Mateo is very busy with the foundation, and Antonio won't look at me, much less talk. I've lost my temper with him a few times. Maya still takes excellent care of the house, but I haven't seen her for several weeks.

I'm in my trailer, going over my lines when Mateo knocks on the door. I specifically asked him to bring me fresh clothes. As he is hanging up my shirts, the door swings open so hard it rattles the trailer.

" Espíritu, we need to talk," the show's director states as he enters the trailer. His face in red with anger. I've seen that a lot lately. He points at Mateo. "Do you want him to leave?"

"No, he can stay," I reply. Mateo continues hanging the shirts.

"I have had it. I don't know what's going on with you, but it can't continue. You have six weeks to get your act together. I'll film the parts of the show that don't include you during that time."

"There's nothing wrong with me," I reply.

"You can't remember your lines. You treat everyone like they are trash beneath your feet, and you're drunk most of the time. Six weeks, Espíritu is all I'm giving you. If you don't straighten this out, I'll either replace you or cancel the show entirely. Either way, you will never work with me or this production company again." He leaves slamming the door behind him.

Mateo turns around and looks at me. "It's time, Matt." I put my head in my hands, knowing Mateo is going to call the last person on earth I want to talk to. My mother.

The following afternoon, I sit on the sofa half buzzed with a glass of whiskey in my hand. The door opens and in walks my mother. Mateo and Antonio follow her, each carrying two suitcases.

"Matthew, you've gotten yourself into a fine mess this time," she says in Spanish, as she walks over to me. She leans down, kisses me on the forehead, and takes the glass from my hand. "Dr. Alcantara will be here tomorrow, but we're going to get a head start." She takes the glass to the kitchen and pours the whiskey down the drain.

"Hello mother," I say. "Nice to see you again."

"Don't get fresh with me and sit up straight." She then opens all the cabinets, searching for liquor bottles. "Mateo, you know what to do!" she says.

Mateo and Antonio leave the room. I know what they are going to do. The two men will turn the entire villa property upside down searching for liquor bottles, beginning with my bedroom.

I just lean back and smile while they go about their business, or rather, my mother's business. I think about Dr. Alcantara. He helped me after **Ama el único camino** when I got lost in Enrique Salas. Dr. Alcantara deprogrammed me and turned me back into Matthew Carson. It was a long process, but now he's only got six weeks to get me back on track, although I don't think I have a problem.

Maya makes a delicious dinner for my mother, Mateo, Antonio, and me. I notice Maya doesn't join us instead; she retreats to her room. The mood is somber, and I gulp my food. Then I go for a swim to ignore my mind's craving for alcohol. I head to bed afterward but cannot sleep because of the lack of alcohol and I'm still missing Vi. I haven't had a good night's sleep since I held her in my arms the last time.

Dr. Alcantara arrives early the next day. He is in his mid-sixties with gray hair and a kind demeanor. He also has the patience of a saint. My mother and he have been seeing each other socially for years and I know she is the only one he would drop everything for to tend to her son.

The doctor's first order of business is to call the TV show director and discuss my issues on the set. Next, he talks to Mateo and Antonio. Finally, he and Mateo come into the living area where I'm lying on the sofa with a terrible headache.

"I would like to talk to Ms. Grimes," Dr. Alcantara says.

"That's not possible. Ms. Grimes refuses to discuss anything related to Matt," Mateo says.

I rise to a sitting position, grabbing my head. "You've talked to Vi?" I ask, surprised.

"Despite everything that's happened, Vi has agreed to continue working with me on foundation business," Mateo answers.

"I want to see her the next time she's in Rome," I state.

Mateo looks at me with pity in his eyes, which angers me. "That's impossible. She only agreed to continue if I guaranteed she would never have to see or talk to you again. Once you're back to running the foundation, I'm sure she will quit." Mateo turns to the doctor. "Rather than talking to her, read her latest book. It pretty much explains everything."

"What book, Mateo?" I ask.

"Her last novel she wrote when she went home. Although she changed things up, anyone that knows of your relationship with her can figure out the story is about the two of you," Mateo states. "Dr. Alcantara, I'll bring you a copy."

"I want to read it too," I demand.

"We'll see," the doctor replies. "We have other matters to attend to first. Mateo, will you bring it to me now?" I roll my eyes and lie back down.

"Mateo, how did her book do?" I ask.

"It hit #1 the first week it became available. Now, if you'll excuse me, I'll get the book and then I have work to do." Mateo turns and leaves.

CHAPTER 33

"Mateo, is now a good time?" I text two weeks later.

"Perfect."

I call Mateo and give him my flight and hotel information. He will meet me at the airport the day after tomorrow and take me to the hotel so I can rest. Mateo gives me the schedule for my three days in Rome. We will tour the newest warehouse, meet with investors and the media, and then talk business, including my thoughts for expansion.

I'll be back on Friday and then pack for Los Angeles for a two-month book tour, thanks to Veronica. This tour will be harder because Grace is seven months pregnant, so we are limiting her travel. Almost everything will be done through shipping back and forth.

The tour will end in New York City again for the awards ceremony. They nominated me again in two categories. Even though Veronica got two tickets for me, I haven't decided to go. I bought a dress though. It differs totally from the red one I wore last year with Matt. Crap! It seems my life these days is categorized into before, during, and after Matt. I'm sick of it. Anyway, the evening gown is matte black and covers me from my neck to my hands to my feet. No skin will show this time.

It's so good to see Mateo again. He's huge, inked arms wrap around me in a tight hug and tears come to my eyes. I've missed him. He drops me off at the hotel, gives me a copy of tomorrow's itinerary, and says he will pick me up at 9:00 am.

When I lie down in bed, an idea occurs to me. I know Veronica sent the tickets to the awards show to Grace. I text Grace and ask her to send me a picture of one ticket.

After a quick breakfast in the hotel's restaurant, I'm waiting in the lobby when Mateo arrives. I smile, seeing him in his blue suit. I know it is the one his parents gave him. As we drive to the first facility, we talk about Mateo's parents. They haven't been back to Rome since his birthday. He tells me now is a bad time for them to visit. I don't ask questions because I don't want to know the answers.

After touring the new facility with investors and medical company personnel, Mateo and I head to the new warehouse and meet with media people. Mateo arranged everything. It was an immense success. The warehouse will be ready for occupancy in two months and there's already a waiting list for residents.

We have dinner at a restaurant near my hotel and discuss the financial operations and expenditures of the foundation. Neither one of us nor Matt draws a salary or uses foundation money for expenses. Everything is out of pocket for us.

The following day, Mateo comes to the hotel to discuss my ideas for expansion for the foundation. I tell him I want to expand to the US. The downturn in the economy the last five years has caused shops to close or move out of shopping centers. These vacant shopping centers would be ideal for a facility and renovation expenses would be less expensive. Mateo likes the idea and tells me to look into it. I smile and tell him I already have.

Because of a prior commitment, Mateo cannot take me to the airport the next day. I reach into my tote bag and pull out a first edition of my latest book.

"Vi, thank you so much. I enjoyed it, but it also generated mixed emotions."

I pat his hand. "I understand. Now, open the book."

"What's this?" Mateo asks, holding up the copy of the ticket.

"I'm asking you to be my date for the awards show."

"Really, Vi? You want me there?"

"Yes, I really do. You enjoyed it last year and I would love for you to attend with me," I reply.

"I would love to."

"Great. You can contact Grace about the arrangements because I'm going on a two-month book tour. Grace won't be able to go this year. She's pregnant."

We talk about Grace for a few minutes. My flight tomorrow is early, so Mateo hugs me tightly and leaves.

CHAPTER 34

Dr. Alcantara is a taskmaster. After he read Vi's book in half a day, we started directly into his program. He insisted I keep a journal. I need to record what we talk discuss, my feelings about the show and my character. I also need to write about my feelings about Vi and her loss. This is something new for me, but everything I write is honest and open. My relationship with Vi was until I screwed up. The part about Vi hurts me in a way I never thought possible.

I am not allowed to drink alcohol or have any contact with the outside world. All the clothing and jewelry I started wearing are gone. Mateo and Antonio transformed one bedroom in the villa into a mini gym. Not Vi's bedroom, though. I demanded it stay the same as the day she left. I am required to work out twice a day for at least one hour each time. My mother and Maya plan and make healthy meals for us to help build up my strength.

For five weeks, Dr. Alcantara and I talk. I yell or I cry while he watches my every move and listens to my every word. It is hard and gut wrenching. Sometimes we laugh, but not very often. Slowly, I feel Matt Carson coming back, but coming back to what, I'm not sure. I do a great deal of soul searching when I'm alone and I don't like what I find, especially in the last eight months of my life.

Wednesday of the fifth week, Dr. Alcantara meets with the TV show's director. He tells him I am ready to return to filming, but that Dr. Alcantara will be with me every day. The director agrees and sends over the script. I'm not surprised the show has been cut to one season and the direction of my character has changed. He also told the doctor that if I can finish out the show with no more problems, he may consider working with me again.

On the last day of the fifth week, I find Vi's book lying on my bed in the afternoon. I've never read one of her books. I'm curious, but hesitant at the same time. There's also a note to record everything I feel as I read the book. After my workout and dinner, I take the book and a new journal to the patio with me and sit by the pool. My mother sticks her head out the door and says everyone will be at the guest house playing games tonight. I wave, knowing the plan was to leave me alone to deal with whatever comes up.

I take a deep breath and open the book. Once past the copyright and the other necessary pages, I find the dedication. It says," **I dedicate this book to the man that taught me true love is an abyss our heart falls into and no matter what happens, my heart will never truly be able to climb out of the abyss that is him**." Vi is talking about me and how deep her love was for me. I wonder if she still feels that way? I write my question in my journal.

As I read the book, I notice the names have changed. To protect the guilty? I smile as I read about when we met, our first sailboat ride, and other things we did. Those are happy memories for me. I read about Vi's struggle to decide whether or not to move in with me. It is almost as if she is sitting beside me, telling me these things.

By this time, I realize it has gotten dark. I don't know what Dr. Alcantara has planned for tomorrow. I should go to bed, but

I can't leave the book. As I continue to read about how Vi's love for me grows, I learn that she always had worries about the differences in our ages while we were together.

As I read, I find Vi talks about the first time we made love and how I made her feel and how wonderful it was. I look away from the book because tears roll down my cheeks. I remember that night so well and always will. Vi also describes other lovemaking sessions. Some really happened, and some didn't. I guess that's how romance novels work.

Making notes in my journal as I read, I am not surprised when she talks about the changes she saw in me. She became concerned about it. Vi discusses how, although we had agreed from the beginning to be open and honest, she felt like I was holding back.

Finally, Vi ends the book with our breakup. What she felt and how she reacted. It breaks my heart to read what I put her through with my selfish actions, and I sob uncontrollably. No wonder she never wants to see or talk to me again. I close the book just as the sun rises. I look at my journal and find that I have filled the entire thing with my thoughts. Finally, I pick up both books, head to my bedroom, and cry myself to sleep.

I wake at noon, shower and dress. I look at myself in the mirror with disgust. When I walk to the kitchen, I find Dr. Alcantara sitting at the island with a cup of coffee and a sandwich waiting for me.

"Where is everyone?" I ask.

"Antonio just left with your mother and Maya to go to Palermo shopping. Mateo left for Rome this morning," he answers, watching me as I eat. "Did you enjoy the book?"

"I enjoyed reading abut the happy times Vi and I had."

"Finish your sandwich. Then get your journal and meet me by the pool," he says, standing and leaving the room. When I finish, I do as he said.

"Sit down, Matt, and tell me what you feel about the end of the book."

"I loathe myself for what I put Vi through. I was selfish and not honest with her."

"Okay, open your journal. We are going to discuss everything you wrote in it," Dr. Alcantara states.

And so we do. I read every page without interruption. I have no idea when Antonio, my mother, and Maya return. The doctor and I stop for dinner when I finish. It's late and everyone has disappeared again.

"Matt, do you want to stop now and continue tomorrow?" Dr. Alcantara asks when we finish dinner.

"No, let's continue by the pool," I answer.

We return to the pool and Dr. Alcantara turns a chair to face mine so he can watch my reactions. I'm used to his tactics by now.

"Matt, do you think your equipment below your waist didn't work because of your feelings toward Vi, or your guilt over what you did?"

"Wow, doc! You started off with a hard question." I pause and take a deep breath. "Honestly, I think both, but my feelings toward Vi are the most. Like I told you, I haven't had a sexual relationship with any woman since Vi."

"Why do you think that is?"

"Because I still love her," I reply, looking down at my lap. "She's the only woman I have ever loved, and I lost her." I cry. I hadn't noticed the box of tissues beside Dr. Alcantara until he hands me several. He lets me cry without interrupting me until I stop.

"Do you want her back?"

"More than anything in this world, but she's moved on."

"Has she Matt? One would wonder about that after reading the dedication," Dr. Alcantara says. "What would you be willing to give up to get her back? Would you continue your career knowing this may happen again? Would you give up your career? I'll let you think about that. Good night, Matt."

I stare at his back as he walks into the house. Next, I get up and wander around the garden with the moon as the only light. Finally, I go to my bedroom and sit on the bed. Curious about Vi, I enter Ivy Webber into a search engine. I find many articles and several videos. Apparently, Vi is on a book tour. I see a video for her first TV interview and click on it.

As the video starts, I notice Vi looks thinner. She also cut her hair shorter with a new style. It looks great. Of course, she is dressed in typical Ivy clothing for the interview. A pencil skirt, heels, and a silky blouse. She sounds like a different person as she talks. Oh, she smiles, of course, but there is no enthusiasm or warmth. Suddenly, Vi leans over to grab her coffee cup and I see it. I pause the video and enlarge the screen. There, tattooed on her left breast, is a small red broken heart. I stare at the tattoo for a long time. Finally, I close my laptop and lie down on the bed where I spend a sleepless night thinking about the questions the doctor asked me. What would I give up to have Vi back?

The following day, Dr. Alcantara informs me we are finished with the deprogramming, but he will stay for a couple of weeks. I pack a bag with several changes of clothes and enough food for three days. I also pack the new script. Antonio and I drop my mother off at the airport. Then Antonio takes me to the sailboat. Without Vi, it takes me several extra minutes for me to get the boat away from the dock.

I spend the next three days learning the script and thinking about Dr. Alcantara's question. I know I love Vi and will never love another woman the way I love her, and I know she completes me. When I return home, I've made a decision. Somehow, I have to see Vi. Just see her. That's all I need and maybe then I can see where my heart leads me. Searching the internet again, I find her schedule and make a plan.

CHAPTER 35

B y the time I reach New York City and my hotel, I'm exhausted. Thankfully, I arrive the day before the awards ceremony and sleep for twelve hours. After a hearty breakfast, I head to the spa to get ready for the ceremony. Mateo texted and said he will be at my hotel at 7:00 pm. I'm excited to see him and look forward to a night spent with a good friend.

It's weird not to have Grace with me, but I received a message from her husband while I was at the spa. They are at the hospital awaiting the birth of their baby. He said Grace is hoping the baby will come soon so the three of them can watch the show.

Mateo arrives on time and looks for handsome in his tux. I can tell he's excited. He asks what he can do to help, and I tell him I need a couple of things from my purse to put into my clutch.

"Vi, what's this?" Mateo asks, walking into my bedroom as I finish applying my lipstick.

"What?" I turn around to find him holding my prescription bottle. I look down. "It helps me not to feel," I say. Mateo says nothing. He just turns and leaves.

I can tell Mateo is excited as the romance novel categories finally arrive. I wasn't nominated for the book cover category this year because I didn't have the heart to design one. Veronica nudges me and points to my clutch. I pull my phone out to find a message that baby Ivy has entered the world and is now napping as her parents watch the show. Usually tears would come to my eyes at the news, but my medication does an excellent job of numbing my emotions.

"And the winner of the romance novel of the year is Ivy Webber!"

Everyone applauds, but it takes a nudge from Mateo to make me realize I'm the winner. I walk to the stage, accept the award, and go to the podium.

"Thank you. My best friend and exceptional personal assistant, Grace, and her husband cannot be here tonight to share this moment with me. So, I want to start off my saying hello to the newest addition to their family, Ivy, who was born two hours ago." The crowd goes wild and I smile. Then I go into all the typical thank you's and encourage the up-and-coming novelists before taking my seat.

"The winner for the book of the year award goes to Ivy Webber!"

Oh, my gosh. Veronica and I walk to the stage, holding hands. I let her speak first. Then it's my turn and unplanned words pour from my mouth after I say thank you again.

"Everyone, I have something to share with you. As you know, I have been working with a foundation for over a year now. This foundation has become very important to me. So not only will all the book sales go to the foundation, but I am taking a break from writing to bring the foundation's dream to the US. I can't say if the break is temporary or permanent because I have yet to decide." I receive a standing ovation. After the crowd calms, I look toward the back of the building and see the unmistakable emerald eyes staring at me. They unnerve me but make me tingle inside. I take a deep breath.

"I have one last person I would like to thank," I say, staring at Matt. "I want to thank the unnamed man that gave me the inspiration for this book. Please bear with me as I repeat the dedication." I never take my eyes off of Matt as I recite the dedication by heart.

"**I dedicate this book to the man that taught me true love is an abyss our heart falls into and no matter what happens, my heart will never truly be able to climb out of the abyss that is him**." Instead of returning to my seat, I walk behind the curtain to the back of the stage. I am shaking and sit my award down quickly for fear of dropping it. Seconds later, Mateo and Veronica are at my side.

"Vi, are you okay? What happened?" Mateo asks, very concerned.

"He was here," is all I can get out.

"Are you sure? He was home when I left yesterday." I nod and faint.

I don't know how long I've been out, but when I come to, I'm in the limo with Mateo's arms around me. "How are you feeling, Vi?" he says, handing me a glass of water.

"A little weak, but okay," I answer.

"You scared Veronica and me."

"I'm sorry Mateo."

'It's okay Vi. I'm going to take you to the hotel. Veronica will meet us there and help you into bed."

Veronica beat us to the hotel and is waiting for us in the
lobby. The three of us go to my room, where Veronica helps
me undress and get into bed. Mateo comes in and says
he will sleep on the sofa in case I need anything. I say
it's unnecessary, but he insists, placing a soft kiss on my
forehead before telling me good night.

CHAPTER 36

"What the hell, Matt?" Mateo texts.

"What?" I reply.

"What were you doing at the award ceremony?"

"I had to see her. I just had to."

"Well, she saw you and it upset her to the point she fainted."

"Is she okay?"

"Yes, she's in her bed. I'm on the sofa in her suite in case she needs anything. I don't understand. You were home when I left yesterday."

"It's a quick trip. I'm at the airport now, waiting to go back home."

"Matt, she's not the same person you remember. She's very fragile and on medication," Mateo says.

"I noticed that when I watched her TV interview. What kind of medication?" I ask.

"A high dose anti-depressant. She says it helps her not to feel."

"Then get her off it. I need her to feel."

I turn my phone to airplane mode before Mateo can reply and head to the bedroom of the chartered plane to sleep. When I close my eyes, I reflect on the past two months.

My first day back at work was hard. Dr. Alcantara stood beside me as I tearfully apologized to everyone involved in the TV series. I explained I wanted to do my best with my character and thus became him in real life. Also, my problems were increased because of personal issues. Everyone said they accepted my apology, but it has taken time for them to warm up to me. Some might never reach that forgiveness point. Dr. Alcantara left two weeks later.

Everyone on the set worked hard to catch up on the gaps my absence caused. We are now early, according to the director. I go home every night and hold each person I work with at arm's length. I work out every morning and eat healthy with no more alcohol. There's not even beer in the house for Sunday soccer games.

Now, I have to think about my future. My mind wanders to Vi. I love her and miss her so much my heart fills empty. When I saw her tonight, she looked as beautiful as ever, even with the evening gown covering her entire body. I wonder if that was intentional. When she looked at me, though, her eyes looked vacant. Perhaps it is the medication that does that. I'll have to ask Mateo what she's taking so I can look up the side effects.

We have one month until we finish the series. Mateo and Antonio have been working on moving from the villa back to the apartment in Rome. The foundation now has two facilities up and running there, whereas there's only one in Madrid. Perhaps it is time to move back to Madrid. I've been offered another TV series but am still considering my options. Dr. Alcantara's questions still run through my mind constantly.

"Do you want her back? What would you be willing to give up to get her back? Would you continue your career knowing this could happen again? Would you give up your career for Vi?"

I know I want Vi back, but would she want me back? What would I have to do to get her back? These are additional questions I ponder every night as I lie in bed. My mom told me to follow my heart when she left. I just don't know how.

CHAPTER 37

A lot has changed in four months. I'm busier than ever with the foundation. I've rented office space and Grace and the baby come in every day to help me. The shopping center facility is almost ready and applications for residents are coming in. I'm in the process of considering another shopping center in Oklahoma City. All the medical staff has been hired, and we have signed a contract with a food service company. I lean back in my chair to take a deep breath.

"Vi, you need to come see this," Grace yells from the other room. She sounds excited. I walk in to find her on her laptop watching a news channel.

"Breaking news from Rome," the announcer states. "Espíritu Libre, the handsome Spanish actor and star of several TV shows in Europe, announced today he is putting his career on hold for the time being. During an interview with our affiliate in Rome, Libre said he wanted to devote more time to his foundation. He also has pressing personal business he needs to resolve."

"Oh, wow!" Grace says. "More time with the foundation. I wonder what that means for you?"

"I don't know. Hopefully, he'll leave me alone. Mateo knows about the work I've been doing and totally supports it," I say and return to my office.

Crap, I think. Just when things are going so well. I'm off my medication and doing well. I can even breath now without my heart breaking every time I hear his name. My phone pings. It's Mateo.

"Hi Vi. Matt is demanding a board meeting tomorrow at 9:00 am our time. See you then."

What the heck? That means midnight tonight my time. Well, that figures. A board meeting. We haven't met as a board in over a year. And, to top that off, Matt supposedly wants to be more involved. I roll my eyes. Well, no time to think about it now. I pick up my purse and leave for a meeting with a realtor in Oklahoma City.

It's 10:00 pm when I return home. I shower, change into my pajamas, and make a sandwich. I have that stupid meeting in an hour. Jotting down my notes I recorded to my phone, I'm almost ready. I power up my laptop, turn the camera off, and mute my volume. Mateo texts me.

"Are you ready?"

"Yes, but I'm having laptop and phone issues. I'll be able to hear what' said, but I'll have to text you my responses." I know Mateo can read between the lines, but he doesn't respond.

"Good evening, Vi. I'm sorry the meeting is so late for you, but we have important things to cover," Matt says, very business-like and cold. Hearing his voice after so long shatters my heart all over again. I take deep breaths and don't respond.

"If you haven't heard by now, I've put my career on hold to get more involved in the foundation," he says. I send Mateo a thumb up emoji. "I have decided that since we have two facilities up and running in Rome, it is time to go back to

Madrid and build another one there." Matt's voice sounds so cold.

"Are you there, Vi?" I send Mateo another thumb up.

"Mateo says you have made great strides in the US. The facility in Tulsa is almost ready to open and you are meeting with a real estate agent in Oklahoma City. That's great. But there is one issue that upsets me greatly. You know how I feel about allowing pharmaceutical companies using residents for experimental purposes in return for donations."

I take a deep breath. Mateo and I discussed it. I had lawyers draw up legal documents that residents or their guardians have to sign, giving permission for the experimental drugs. I also put a maximum of 50% of the residents would be involved. Tears suddenly come to my eyes. This is Matt's way of calling me out.

I text Mateo. "Tell Matt I will send in my resignation by 8:00 am my time. I will stay until he can find a replacement."

I hearing whispering in the background. Mateo sounds angry. Then Matt says, "I'm sorry you feel that way, Vi. I would be happy to interview any prospects you suggest for your replacement. Please send their names ASAP. Mateo and I will be in Tulsa within a week to tour the new facility before it opens. Good bye."

I close my laptop and throw my phone on the sofa. How dare he do this to me after all my hard work? Does he hate me that much? Or do I hate him that much? No, I'm still in love with him, which makes leaving the foundation even harder. Although I hadn't seen or talked to him in a year or so, it was still a tie to him. I cry my heart out and when I finish. Then I type up a very professional resignation letter and email it to Matt and Mateo.

CHAPTER 38

"Well, that didn't go as planned, you idiot," Mateo says as I hang my head in my hands.

"No, I never expected her to resign. I know how much she loves the foundation. She must really hate me," I reply.

"She doesn't hate you, Matt. Vi's still in love with you and always will be. It's just her way of coping with the pain. What's your next plan? I hope it's better."

"We're going to show up in Tulsa unexpectedly. If Vi has knowledge of our visit, she'll send Grace to give us the tour."

Mateo smiles weakly. "When do you want to go?"

"Let's leave before her resignation letter gets here," I answer.

"That's in seven hours. I guess we better pack. I call the pilot to get the plane ready." As Mateo presses numbers on his phone, I go to pack my bag.

Mateo and I land in Tulsa at 2:00 pm, the following day, check into our hotel and nap until 3:30. We shower and dress, then drive to the new facility. It is 4:55 and Mateo texts Grace that we are at the facility and ready for our tour. In my mind, I can see Vi rolling her eyes and saying a few choice words, not only because we surprised her, but it's pouring rain. I smile.

Fifteen minutes later, Vi pulls up to the front door. I notice a magnetic sign on her vehicle for the foundation. It warms my heart. She opens the door and struggles with her umbrella. Mateo walks over to help her while I stand under the driveway awning and watch.

"Thanks for the advanced notice," Vi says when she and Mateo walk up. She keeps her head down and refuses to look at me. I ignore her comment and wait for her to unlock the door because I deliberately waited until all the workers were gone.

Vi turns the lights on and the building lights up with pastel colors and a ceiling painted to represent the sky.

"Where shall we begin?" I ask as loud thunder rolls across the sky. "I would like to see the blueprints, too."

"I don't have them with me, but I'll go back and get them while the two of you look around," Vi replies.

"I'll go get them. No point in you getting soaked, Vi," Mateo says and leaves.

"We can start down here," Vi says, pointing to one end of the shopping center. I follow her, taking everything in. She has done a marvelous job designing the interior. When we reach the end, Vi says, "this was a cafeteria before they closed down. The company just replaced all the appliances before closing down. Everything is in working order, which saved the foundation quite a bit. As you can see, it's large enough to accommodate up to 100 people."

The place is spotless and there are more than enough tables and chairs stacked against one wall. "I had planned to have the grand opening festivities here," Vi says, and I detect sadness in her voice. "I signed the food service contract last week to provide three meals per day, plus snacks in the morning and afternoon. All healthy, of course." She still refuses to look at me.

"Impressive," I say as a loud siren sounds. "What's that?"

"Tornado warning. We need to take shelter. Come with me." I follow Vi to the middle of the shopping center. She opens a door, lets me in first, turns a light on, and locks the door behind us.

"What's this room?"

"It's the safe room. We have tornadoes in the area this time of year. I reinforced the walls and ceiling with twelve inch steel. There's room for 100 people. I stocked the closet over there with chairs, cots, water, and snacks."

"You already have snacks in here?"

"I had to make sure the workers were taken care of. If a tornado were to hit, there's no telling how long someone has to stay in here until help arrives," Vi answers. "Safety of the residents and workers is one of my priorities."

"I'm very impressed, Vi. You always cared so much about everyone else's welfare. Good job," I say, but she still won't look at me. I walk around and look in the storage closet. I observe they also painted the ceiling to look like the sky and the walls look like a park, complete with trees, flowers, and various plants. "Did you do this?"

Vi laughs a little. "I designed it, but someone else had to paint it."

I look at my watch. "Mateo should be back by now. I'll call him."

"Cell phones won't work here. If he doesn't see us, he'll know where we are. He has a key to the room."

Suddenly, a phone rings, and Vi walks over to the door. She opens a panel and answers the phone. "Mateo, we're fine. We are in the safe room. Oh, that's terrible. I understand. We'll be fine. I brought in water and snacks last week. Don't worry about us." Vi pauses. "Please be careful and stay safe." She hangs up the phone.

"What did he say?" I ask noticing concern on her face.

"The area has been hit by a tornado and more are predicted. The streets are impassible, so Mateo can't get here. We are not the first responders priority since we're okay. Mateo has volunteered to help with search and rescue. We'll be fine, Matt. Mateo will call when it's safe to leave the room."

Vi finally said my name. My heart jumps. She walks over to the closet and retrieves a chair for each of us. "How long will that be?"

"It could be all night. I didn't listen to the weather forecast before I came," Vi answers, handing me a chair. I get a whiff of her familiar vanilla and cinnamon scent and my heart aches to touch her and breath the scent in off her hair and shoulder. Instead, we sit in silence for several minutes about five feet apart.

"Why do you hate me, Matt? I did nothing to you to deserve your hatred?"

Talk about a punch in the gut. I hold my breath for a few seconds. Well, I guess it's now or never. "I don't hate you, Vi. I love you." There! It's out in the open.

For the first time since I arrived, Vi looks at me. "Then why did you accept my resignation?"

"I didn't accept it. As far as I'm concerned I haven't received it yet. I haven't checked my email since yesterday. I don't plan to accept it."

Vi looks at me, confused. "Why didn't you tell me that last night?"

"I wanted to teach you a lesson because I want you to think with your heart, not your hatred for me," I reply. "You love the foundation, I know that, but I also know you wouldn't want to work with me."

Vi looks down at her lap. She draws circles on her thigh. A thigh I would love to kiss. "I don't hate you, Matt. I can never hate you, no matter how badly you hurt me."

I move my chair closer to her so I can reach her, but I don't touch her. She's not ready for that. "I know I hurt you and I wish it had never happened. I'm very sorry, Vi."

"I thought we were happy, and I was enough for you," she says as a tear slips down her cheek.

"You were, and you still are. I guess I better explain. When I became an actor, I wanted to be believable. It started with **Ama el único camino**. Perhaps, it was because it was 140 episodes and filming lasted three years. I became the character. I lived, breathed, and loved like Enrique Salas. I dressed like him, talked like him, even walked like him after the show was over. My mother and Mateo became concerned because I wasn't Matt Carson anymore. Enrique had a more exciting life than I did and I craved the excitement and the women, to be honest." I stop and take a deep breath before continuing. I look at Vi to see if there's any understanding in her eyes.

"My mother has a close friend that's a retired psychiatrist. She called him and he came to the clinic. It took three months of intense therapy to get me back to the real me. Deprogramming, the doctor called it. Everything was back to normal. I hated it when I had to dress like Enrique and wear the jewelry. I still do, but like I told you, that's what the public fell in love with and expects."

Vi looks at me. "I remember you telling me that."

I nod and continue. "You and I met, and I immediately fell in love with you. Everything was perfect. You were perfect. You and I on the sailboat, dressing like tourists wandering around Rome, the impromptu picnics, dancing in the rain, everything. Then you moved in and I learned what it would be like to have a life partner. Then we started filming the new show. I loved coming home to you and waking up with you. I loved our nights together." The phone rings and Vi gets up to answer it.

"Mateo, are you alright? Oh, that's good news." Vi listens for a minute and tears come to her eyes. "Okay, Mateo, I understand. Thank you for letting me know. We'll see you soon."

"Vi, what's happened?" I walk over to her as tears run down her cheeks.

"Grace and her family are okay. The office is okay, but," Vi sobs. "My apartment is gone. There's nothing left of the building. Several people that were in the building were killed."

Without hesitation, I wrap her in my arms and let her cry on my shoulder. It's poor timing, but she feels so good in my arms again. I hold her tightly for a long time. Then Vi backs away from me. I wipe her tears away.

"Matt, please finish your story. We're going to be here for a while."

I lead her back to our chairs and continue. "Well, again, I wanted to be the best and make my character believable. People on the set knew you and I were living together, but we never made it official or public. People started showing up with alcohol to have a relaxing drink after work. Women were constantly flirting with me. I was becoming the character again. As you know, I was dressing like him and everything else. I began to forget about you as my life partner and I started ignoring you and the wonderful life we had together. Then I told you what I did about other women."

"I overheard you and Mateo arguing that night. I didn't understand what that was about," Vi says quietly.

"Mateo is like a brother to me. He saw the signs just like the first time. I wish I had listened to him earlier. Anyway, I didn't know you had left. Mateo took me to work the next morning. I stayed in the trailer for two nights partying with people from the show. Then I went home. That's when I discovered you were gone. The house had been totally cleaned from top to bottom. It was as if you had never been there. Then I found the jewelry I gave you, including the commitment ring. Instead of going to bed, I drove back to the trailer." My mouth is parched. I don't know if it's from all the talking I've done or the guilt I feel. I go to the closet and get each of us a bottle of water. I gulp the whole thing down.

"Please continue, Matt."

"I drank more and more. I tried to sleep with other women, but it didn't work because I couldn't perform. I thought it was from the alcohol, but in reality, I was in love with you and only wanted to be with you." Pausing, I look at Vi, wanting some type of reaction, but she is staring at her bottle of water.

"Anyway, I was spiraling out of control because I couldn't stop drinking and couldn't remember my lines. I mistreated everyone on the set badly. I would only go home once or twice a week to get fresh clothes. Mateo, Antonio, and Maya avoided me. Then one day, while Mateo was there delivering fresh clothes, the director came in and he was furious. He said I had six weeks to get myself back together. He said if I didn't he would either replace me or cancel the show completely. Mateo heard it all. When the director left, Mateo called my mother. She came the next day and the same doctor that had worked with me before came the following day."

"I think you need a break," is all Vi says. "It's safe to leave the room. Let's go look outside."

I follow her out of the room to the front door, and we step outside. It looks worse than a war zone. Vi's car is upside down, sitting across the street, almost unrecognizable. People are walking around bleeding, holding broken bones. Others are screaming the names of family or friends they can't find. I tell Vi to stay there and walk around the entire building. When I return, she is sitting on the curb staring at the devastation.

"The building is fine," I tell her. "I saw no damage, not even a broken window."

"That's good news. If it's okay with you, I'll see what the foundation can do to help before I leave. It's going to take years to rebuild this neighborhood."

"Vi, I don't want you to quit the foundation. I want you to stay and we'll work together."

"We'll see. Come with me." Vi stands and I follow her as walks over to a first responder.

"Excuse me," she says. She points at me. "Our foundation owns the old shopping center. We are offering it as a shelter. We have 100 cots, some water, and snacks."

The burly firefighter grabs Vi and hugs her tightly. "Ma'am, thank you so much. There's no other place around her large enough to accommodate these people. I'll call it in and get our organizations to bring more supplies."

Vi turns to me. "The only room with power is the safe room and will be for several days. You go set up the cots and I'll invite the people in." I nod, hug her, and kiss her on the forehead. My Vi. Always thinking of others.

CHAPTER 39

It's been a long week. Matt, Mateo, and I have had very little sleep. After talking to the firefighter, Matt set up the cots and got the water and snacks out while I encouraged people to come inside. Two hours later, vehicles from various organizations showed up with more water, sandwiches, and blankets. Mateo showed up an hour later with medical supplies and a pastor from a local church. We were up all night tending to minor injuries. People from the unaffected areas of the city brought what they could. We had a room for clothes and shoes, diapers, baby formula and bottles, pet food, and other essentials.

I'm not sure of the capacity of the shopping center, but every room was full of people. We separated families into one area and single people in another. We welcomed pets as well, and we had some strange ones, too. I stayed away from the snakes. LOL.

The following day, an organization with a huge trailer showed up providing hot meals. Another brought in washers and dryers and did laundry for people. Grace and her husband left the baby with Grace's parents and came to help. Bless her, she brought me some clothes since we're the same size.

Two days later, a commercial construction company delivered a massive generator. It looked half the size of the shopping center, along with a fuel truck. Thank goodness the contractor insisted on installing the ductwork and vents early in the construction phase. The generator didn't cool the building entirely, but it made it more bearable.

Insurance companies set up shop in the parking lot with temporary buildings. Everyone pitched in and helped. It was very rewarding to the community, city, and outsiders come together. Several investors and donors in the foundation sent money to help take care of everyone. Veronica, her brother, and their spouses even flew in to help.

Matt, Mateo, and I had a board meeting in a corner and decided to keep the shelter open for a month. Then we would re-assess the situation. We also took turns going to Matt and Mateo's hotel to shower and nap.

By the second week, things slowed down, and some people left. They moved in with family or friends or their insurance company found them temporary housing. We still had many people to take care of. It was heartbreaking watching heavy equipment tear down damaged homes and clear the neighborhood. Every day, I cried in the shower when I went to the hotel to take my turn for a rest period.

At the beginning of the third week, we were at half the capacity we were when we started. An amiable man approached me while I was taking a break in the parking lot.

"Ms. Grimes, I'm Bill Jensen. According to our records, you lost your apartment and all your belongings in the storm."

"I guess that's true. I haven't been there, so I only know what my friends have told me."

"Well, I'm with your insurance company. I've been there several times with Mr. Carson and his friend. You and I need to talk about a place to stay and a settlement for your belongings."

"Mr. Jensen, I appreciate your concern, but I just can't deal with it now. I'm a little overwhelmed at the point."

"Ms. Grimes, I understand. My company and I appreciate all your foundation's work and generosity to your community. I'll be here for at least another week." He turns and walks off.

I feel a warmth come over my body and turn around to find Matt standing a foot away.

"What was that about?" he asks.

I laugh. "My insurance settlement. He said you and Mateo were there with him."

"Yes, and I found something that belongs to you." Matt opens his hand, revealing a small box. I know what's in it. My parents' wedding rings. I sob from happiness, sadness, and exhaustion.

Matt lifts me, carries me to the car, and puts me inside. Once he's inside, he calls Mateo and tells him we are going to the hotel and will be back sometime tomorrow. I'm still sobbing when we reach the hotel room. I'm too tired to protest when Matt undresses both of us and steps into the shower. He tenderly bathes me and washes my hair. After drying us both, he carries me to the bed and climbs in beside me. He takes me in his muscular arms and we both fall asleep.

I wake up hot, uncovered, naked, and wrapped in Matt's arms. I do not know how I got here, but I feel clean and refreshed. Raising my head slightly, I see Matt's still sleeping and for the first time; I look at him. I mean, I really look at him since I left. Matt's hair is much shorter, probably just touches his collar. He's shaved his beard, leaving only his mustache and goatee. I see the beginnings of crow's feet around his eyes. My heart aches at the sight of him. Lord, I love this man so much and he says he loves me, but how can I be sure? Can I let my guard down and open my heart again? I turn on my back and close my eyes. Then, Matt pulls the bedcovers over me, covering my nakedness.

"Hello, Vi," he says in his sleepy gruff that makes me tingle all over. Matt touches my tattoo. "I did that, didn't I?" Is voice is sad.

"Yes, but there were two others before you, remember?" I reply. How did I get here?" I ask, waving my hand across the room.

"It's not important. You've had a shower and rested. That's all that matters."

"What time is it?" I feel Matt turn away from me to look at his phone.

"It's 3:00 pm. We've slept almost twelve hours." I look around for something to cover myself so I can get out of bed. I see a robe laying across a chair on the other side of the room. Oh, well. It's not like Matt hasn't seen me naked before.

As I throw back the bedcovers and start to get up, Matt grabs my arm. "What's the hurry?"

"I need to get back to the center."

"It can wait a little while. Mateo texted two hours ago and said everything was fine and not to rush."

I plump up the pillows and lean back against them. "Okay, what do we do now?" I ask, not looking in his direction.

"Well," he sighs. "Would you like to hear the rest of my story?" I shrug, so he plumps his pillows and leans back as well. "I only had six weeks, so Dr. Alcantara and I had very intense discussions lasting all day and sometimes into the night. Slowly, I felt Matt Carson slowly coming back to life. A great deal of soul searching happened during that time. Then, in the middle of the fifth week, the doctor met with the show's director and told him I was ready to go back to work. The script was sent to me. I was surprised to find the show had been changed from three seasons to one. Also, my character had changed considerably."

"Did your character change for the good?" I ask.

"Yes. Without really knowing me, the scriptwriter changed it into more like a person who Matt Carson wanted, no, needed, to be. At the end of the week, I found your book on my bed, along with a note to write in a journal, which was part of my deprogramming. I took both to the pool and everyone left the house. You know, Vi, until that point, I had never read one of your books. Mateo always told me how great they were, but I just never took the time."

I shrug my shoulders and say, "my books aren't for everyone."

"They should be," Matt says. "You always include some type of motivational message or life lesson in them. I've read them all now." He takes a deep breath. "I started not to read the book, but it kept pulling at me. The dedication took my breath away. I wasn't sure if you were talking about me or someone else. We had been apart for a while. Then I started reading the book. It only took to page two for me to realize the book was about us and your journey into falling in love with me. I relived every happy moment we shared and when I read about how you felt the first time we made love, I cried." Matt's voice falters, but I still won't look at him.

"Vi, you'll never know how special that night was for me. It reinforced all the love I felt for you and I knew I couldn't live without you. Anyway, I stayed up all night reading the book. I didn't know you were noticing changes in me and how you felt I wasn't being open and honest with you like we promised. Then I got to the ending. You were so open about the hurt you felt. It made me sick to know I did that to you."

I can't help the bitterness that fills my mind and I say, "it's water under the bridge now. Neither one of us can change what happened."

"That's true, Vi. Anyway, I filled an entire journal while I was reading your book. I brought it along in the hope you would read it. Perhaps it will explain things better than I can."

"Are you finished?" I ask.

"Not quite. Will you give me a few more minutes of your time?" Matt asks. I nod. "The next day, the doctor and I discussed my journal and everything in it. There's something important you need to hear. Yes, I told you I wanted to be with other women. I can't deny that happened. Like I told you, I could never perform. It was weird and upsetting at the time, which is another reason I drank more. Through my talk with Dr. Alcantara, I realized that I only wanted to be with you and somehow my love for you prevented me from having sex with others. Vi, you are the last woman I've been with." Matt places his hand under my chin, turning my head so that I have to face him.

"It's extremely difficult for a man to admit he has performance issues, but now that I've realized the reason for it, it makes perfect sense to me. I haven't even had the desire," he says. I search his eyes for the truth for several seconds. There is nothing but pure honesty in Matt's emerald gaze.

"I'm almost finished," Matt says, releasing my chin. I lower my eyes to my lap. "Dr. Alcantara then asked the hardest questions he has ever asked in the years that I've known him. He asked if I wanted you back and what I would give up to get you back, including my career."

I'm afraid to ask, but I have to know. "And what did you decide?"

"I knew I wanted you back, but I did not know what to do or how to do it. To be honest, I still don't. But what would I be willing to give up took a lot of time and thought. One thing I knew was that I needed to see you in the flesh. That's when I showed up at the awards ceremony. I didn't plan on you seeing me, though."

I sigh, "It was a surprise, that's for sure," I say. "It really upset me."

"I know that now, and I'm sorry for that. It wasn't my intention at all. So, finishing my tale of woe, I went back and finished the TV series. That's when I made my decision. I chose you. I announced I was putting my career on hold. I didn't officially retire because I will need to do personal appearances to keep my name and face out there to bring in money for the foundation. But I'm not doing anything long term ever again."

"But Matt, you love to act."

"I love you more and want a life with you, Vi. Do you think we have a chance? Do you think we could start over?" Matt asks.

"I don't know, Matt, because I don't know if I'm strong enough to do it again. I'll have to think long and hard about it."

"Vi, look at me." I do. "Do you still love me?"

"Yes," I whisper. "I never stopped," and then I crawl out of bed.

CHAPTER 40

Vi and I both shower again, eat a hearty meal from room service and head back to the shelter. There are only forty-five people left now. The adults are cleaning the building while the children play in the safe room. The laundry truck and the insurance company representatives are gone. Only the large generator and fuel truck remain. The contractor is waiting for Vi when we return.

"Vi, I need to talk to you about the shopping center in Oklahoma City," the contractor says as Vi and I walk up to him. She nods and waves for Mateo to join us. "There's too much structural damage to the building to make it a workable option for the foundation."

Mateo speaks up then. "The realtor came by and said there's one in Stillwater that's in foreclosure and might work. It's a little smaller, though. It's only an hour away if you want to see it."

"Are you free for a couple of hours?" Vi asks the contractor. He nods. "Okay, Mateo, call the realtor and ask her to meet us there in an hour." Mateo steps away to make the call. After a few minutes, he gives us a thumbs up.

"Let's go in my truck," the contractor says. "Vi, will you sit in front with me? I have something important to discuss with you." Vi and the contractor talk in low voices while Mateo gives me an update on the foundation. We've put it on hold during the tornado crisis.

The realtor meets us at the shopping center in Stillwater, and we tour the facility. It looks promising. The contractor leaves us to do a visual inspection while the rest of us talk about the foreclosure process. Vi falls in love with the building even though the building is smaller and the estimated number of residents will be 15% less than in our other locations.

Vi tells the realtor to get the facility inspected and let us know the results. She and the contractor talk more on the way back to Tulsa. When we say goodbye, Vi tells the contractor to give her two days. He should then have some workers meet at the shopping center at 10:00 am on the third day. Vi spends the night overseeing the shelter while Mateo and I go back to the hotel to sleep and eat.

"Well, how did it go?" Mateo asks as we eat.

"It went well enough, I suppose. I was open and honest with Vi. I told her everything," I reply.

"And?"

"And, she admitted, she still loves me, but needs time to think. She doesn't know if she's strong enough to have a relationship with me again."

"That makes sense. Vi was and still is hurt. Hey, I have an idea. In a week or so, when this is over, why don't you ask Vi to go to Madrid with you to look for a house or an apartment? She has no home to go to and she'll need a break after all this. I think it would do you both good."

"You know, Mateo, that's a good idea, but there are things to do here. It will be hard to get her to agree to go," I say.

"No, it won't. I'll stay here until she gets back. Between Grace and I, we'll find a new place for Vi. You know, let me suggest it instead of you. It might go over better."

"Okay, it's a plan. Good luck. You'll have to be very convincing."

"I'll get Grace to help me. You know, Vi is paying Grace out-of-pocket even though Grace is doing mostly foundation work now. That's something I think we should discuss." I nod in agreement.

When Mateo and I arrive at the shopping center the following morning, I expect Mateo to drive Vi to the hotel. Instead, she asks him to take her to the office. She says she has some work to do that is not foundation related. I don't see Vi until the next morning, when she does the same thing. When I ask if I could help, she replies no.

The third morning, Vi rushes to the hotel to clean up and then is back by 9:00 am. She and the contractor meet behind closed doors. Beginning at 9:45, I see twenty men and women sitting in the room Vi asked Mateo and me to set up for a meeting. Even though Mateo and I weren't invited, we stand at the back of the room when Vi and the contractor enter.

I listen closely as Vi speaks. Apparently, the people remaining at the center work for the contractor in our building. All of them, whether married or single, have lost everything or almost everything to the tornado. They either have no place to live or their homes were severely damaged and need extensive repairs.

Vi begins by telling them she knows they haven't worked since the tornado hit, but they will get their full paychecks tomorrow. Their insurance premiums and 401K contributions have all been paid, so they don't have to worry about that. My heart grows fuller with love as I listen to her.

Next, Vi tells them they will return to work on Monday if they still want the job. The work schedule will be four ten-hour days. The food service company will be on site on Monday to serve three meals per day to all the workers. Vi says arrangements have been made with an extended stay hotel to house everyone until they find another place to live or get their home repaired. All workers will be given an opportunity to chip in to help their fellow workers repair homes and will be paid time and one-half while they work.

Finally, Vi says everyone in the room is welcome to apply to a special fund that was set up. It will provide funds for repairs or replacement of their homes and personal property. Anyone that lost their means of transportation or needs storage facilities should see her after the meeting. She adds there are vehicles parked in front of the building to take them, their families, and belongings to the hotel. "Bill," Vi yells across the room to one worker. "Please don't forget to take your snakes with you when you leave." The entire room laughs.

I look around the room as the meeting comes to a close. Each worker approaches Vi with tears in their eyes and asks if they can hug her. She embraces each one, offers words of encouragement and comfort, and hands them envelopes. Mateo and I both wipe the tears from our eyes as we watch the beautiful woman we have grown to love, each in our own way.

A few hours later, Vi and the contractor emerge from the small room they were using as an office. They met with each worker that required immediate help of some type. The contractor leaves, and Vi and I stand in the center of the building.

"Matt, the building is spotless. You can't tell anything ever happened here."

"I know. Everyone here, including the kids, pitched in to clean the entire facility before they would consider leaving." I reach for her and pull her to me and into my arms. Vi doesn't resist. I know it's because she's tired after being awake for over forty-eight hours. "You are an amazing woman. How did you do it?" I ask.

Vi blushes and looks so cute in her pink tinted face. "I had help. Veronica, her brother, and some of their friends pitched in."

"You promised a great deal. You mind if I ask how much you raised?"

"Well, it was $5M when I left the office this morning with $2M more pledged. Everyone agreed that anything left over could go to the foundation. Now, let's lock up and go to the hotel. I need to sleep."

"Do you want me to call ahead and get you a room?" I ask because she and I had alternated using one room except the twelve hours we slept together.

"Honestly, Matt, I'm too tired to care about something like that right now."

I smile inwardly. "Okay. You go get in the car. Mateo and I will lock up and be there in a few minutes."

After stopping for a meal, Mateo and I drop Vi off at the hotel. Next, we head over to her old apartment building. There has been so much devastation that her building hasn't been touched yet. Together, we dig through the rubble, looking for anything Vi might consider valuable. It's dark when we return to the hotel. Vi's sleeping soundly, so I quietly shower and crawl into bed next to her. I smile as I close my eyes because she is wearing one of my T-shirts.

Chapter 41

I wake up alone and look at my phone for the time. I'm shocked to see that I've slept twenty-four hours. Stretching, I turn on my side to see a box sitting at the foot of the bed. I grab it, pull it to me, and open it. Inside is a treasure trove of memories. There are pictures of my mother and father, the three of us together, and me as a child. There are also pictures of my two husbands and me. A small box contains several pieces of my jewelry and a watch that belonged to my father. It's the watch I gave him for his fifty-fifth birthday. I turn it over and read the inscription I had engraved on the back.

That's when it really hits me. I have lost everything. I sob uncontrollably and in a few seconds, I'm wrapped in muscular arms. Matt holds me tightly, letting me cry my heart out. He never says a word as he strokes my hair.

When my sobs end and the hiccups begin, Matt lies on the bed, taking me with him and never releasing me. I guess I dozed off because when I open my eyes, he's still there cradling me in his arms.

He kisses me on the forehead. "Feel better?"

"Yes, and thank you for my things."

"I wish there was more, Vi, but that's all Mateo and I could find. I'm sorry."

"It's fine. The other things are just material items that can be replaced. These are my memories. They are what matters most. I guess I need to look for a place to live now that the center is closed."

"Vi, I'm glad you brought that up." Matt pauses and continues. "You've been through a lot the last few weeks. I think you need a break."

"A break? Matt, I have no place to live, very few clothes, and no vehicle. I don't have time to take a break. Besides, I have foundation work to do."

"Mateo!" Matt yells, and Mateo enters the room. I adjust the bedcovers to cover myself. "Mateo, Vi says she can't take a break right now."

"Vi, you can take a break. Matt needs to go to Madrid and find a place for us to live. Right now, you have nothing here but Grace. You go with Matt. Grace and I will take care of finding you a place to live and a vehicle. I'll stay here to take care of all the foundation items."

I look between the two men. "Why do I feel the two of you planned this?"

"Actually, I had nothing to do with it," Matt replies. "This is all Mateo's idea. Personally, I think he wants the break from me and is using you as an excuse."

"It would be nice to get away and forget about everything for a few days. When do you plan to leave, Matt?"

"I need to leave tomorrow. There are some pressing foundation issues I need to take care of that I've put aside during this tragedy."

"Oh well, I guess I better get up and go buy some clothes," I state.

"It's taken care of," Matt says, pointing to the other side of the room. "Whatever you don't like, Grace will return."

The following morning, Mateo drops Matt and me at the airport. After checking in, we buy coffee and I buy a book to read, dropping it into my new tote bag. Matt and I talk about the type of residence he wants to find. He says he loved the pool, garden, and view the villa had, so perhaps a house instead of an apartment. The location just has to be close to docks so he can have his sailboat nearby.

Because Matt booked the flights late, his first class cubicle is in the last row and mine at the front. While we are waiting for the rest of the passengers to board, my phone pings with an email. He has forwarded my email containing my resignation letter along with a message that says denied. I smile and shake my head.

After takeoff, they serve us a meal. Then I settle back to read. I reach into my tote to grab my book but find three journals with a note that says please read in order. Matt has them marked one, two, and three. I place my headphones on to block the noise of the plane and begin to read on our long non-stop flight to Madrid.

As I read, I laugh and cry. The first journals give me insight into the man Matt was then and his hopes and dreams as an actor. Reading the first two journals, I can better understand how he let his character take over his life. But it's the last journal he wrote while reading my book that turns my world upside down.

In the journal, Matt talks about his views of the happy times we shared and how they made him feel. He writes about falling in love with me and patiently giving me time to fall for him. Matt discusses in detailed honesty about the difference in our ages and how he isn't concerned. He just wants to share whatever time we have together.

The last half of the journal discusses our breakup. Matt knows he broke my heart, but what I didn't know was the heartbreak he experienced. He never expressed his feelings holding them inside until the doctor made him discuss them during his deprogramming.

The last part of the journal is about Matt's hopes and dreams for the future. He desperately desires a future with me and does not know how to accomplish it after hurting me so badly. Matt talks about giving up his career for me and the two of us, along with Mateo, expanding the foundation's work to other countries. Matt ends the journal with a prayer asking God to show him the way.

I wipe the tears from my eyes for the last time as the pilot announces we are beginning our descent into Madrid. I lean back and close my eyes. Now, I know the man that is Matthew Carson better. My heart swells with pride, knowing how much he has been through and came out on the other side. I go to the lavatory to clean myself up, so I won't look horrendous for Matt when we land.

I only intended to stay for one week, but it has turned out to be two months. Matt finally found a home on the coastline of Portugal outside a small town named Vila Nova De Gaia. The town is beautiful and colorful and the people are friendly. The dock is only two miles away. Matt opted for a smaller place with three bedrooms because Antonio wanted to stay in Madrid close to his family. Maya decided to stay in Rome, close to her family. The house should be ready to move into in three weeks.

Matt bought another three-bedroom house nearby along the coastline for Mateo as a gift for being such a loyal friend. It's time for Mateo to find a woman and settle down, Matt said with a laugh. Also, becoming more of a private person rather than a public figure, Matt won't need Mateo as a bodyguard as often. The three of us will continue working on the foundation.

Mateo has been in touch with me several times, saying he and Grace have been unsuccessful in locating a new apartment for me because of the tornado. I know that's not true because I've searched for apartments in and around Tulsa online.

Matt and I've been furniture shopping and spending a great deal of time together. He patiently waited for me to trust him again and love him in every way possible.

My phone rings while Matt and I relax around the hotel pool in Madrid. I answer and put the phone on speaker.

"Hi Mateo."

"Hi Vi. I just wanted to let you know Grace and I still haven't found a place for you."

I reach over and take Matt's hand. "That's okay, Mateo. I don't need a place in Tulsa anymore."

"Really? That's wonderful news. Then I'll be flying to Madrid on Friday," he says excitedly.

"Mateo," Matt says. "You'll have to find your own hotel. Vi and I will be on our honeymoon, sailing the boat from Sicily to Portugal."

"That's amazing news," Mateo yells. "But Portugal?"

"I'll explain when we see you. Goodbye, Mateo. I need to take care of my fiancé now," Matt says, disconnecting the call. "Come, woman, it's time for a nap." I giggle because I know sleeping is the last thing on his mind, or mine, for that matter.

About the Author

Gaylene Nunn is a retired 60+ year old woman who spent my career in banking, financial services, municipal government, and most recently as CFO for a upper level regional university that she helped create. She retired in 2017 with the title of Vice President Emeritus. She is the author of "Before Your Loved Ones Goes ... Planning for Your Reality", "A Second Chance for Love", "Forty Years too Late?", "Love Can Heal" and "Reclaimed Affirmation".

Also By

Love Can Heal

A Second Chance at Love

Reclaimed Assurance

Forty Years too Late?

Before Your Loved One Goes—Planning for Your Reality

*Damaged by Love

*An Eternity of Love

*Co-authored with Deserie LaCrosse

www.ingramcontent.com/pod-product-compliance
Lightning Source LLC
Chambersburg PA
CBHW070753160726
48004CB00001B/173